Table of Contents

1. Burden or Sacrifice 1
   Ameria Lewis
2. Daughter of Thorns 19
   Hope Erica Schultz
3. Cold Bargain 31
   Jeanne Kramer-Smyth
4. A Princess, a Mission, and a Kiss 46
   Lori Bond
5. Princess Deneige 68
   Susan Bianculli
6. Becoming 92
   Kath Boyd Marsh
7. So the Story Goes 118
   Christine Mariniak
8. The Princess and the P 141
   Steve DuBois
9. Aurora in the Dreaming 164
   Alison Ching
10. Redemption 191
    Madeline Smoot

Perilous Princesses

Susan Bianculli Lori Bond
Alison Ching Steve DuBois
Jeanne Kramer-Smyth Ameria Lewis
Christine Marciniak Kath Boyd Marsh
Hope Erica Schultz Madeline Smoot

CBaY Books
Dallas, Texas

Perilous Princesses
Edited by Madeline Smoot

Text Copyright © 2018
Castle Background Copyright © shutterstock.com/
Maxi_M
Princess 1 Copyright © shutterstock.com/Ataly
Princess 2 Copyright © shutterstock.com/SusIO
Weapons Copyright © shutterstock.com/Santi0103

All rights reserved. This book may not be reproduced in any manner whatsoever without express permission of the copyright holder.
For more information, write:
CBAY Books
PO Box 670296
Dallas, TX 75367

Children's Brains are Yummy Books
Dallas, Texas
www.cbaybooks.com

ISBN: 978-1-944821-36-4
eBook ISBN: 978-1-944821-37-1
Kindle ISBN: 978-1-944821-38-8
PDF ISBN: 978-1-944821-39-5

Burden or Sacrifice

Ameria Lewis

I listened to the susurration of the ship-wrought waves washing back against the hull, the hiss of metal prow cleaving through the calm waters of the navy blue sea. The sound once calmed me, mesmerized me. Once, I thought life aboard ship was a luxury.

I am wiser now, and my love for the ocean has turned into resentment for the prison it has become. I wander the open water aboard a luxurious ship because I have no home on land. I have no welcome in any kingdom or democracy. On the sea, I am believed powerless. On land? On land, I am a goddess, and I made the mistake of letting my power be known.

What would you have done, faced with what I faced? What would you have done, with your home under attack, all you loved burnt and poisoned? What would you have done, seeing your parents brought to their knees and forced to beg not for their lives, but for yours?

You would have done as I did and raised the earth to bury the intruders. Whipped the winds and brought down lightning to strike at those invaders who had no place being in your homeland. You would have brought the melted rock from deep below to the surface to burn them all to ash.

I saved them all, my parents, my people. For that, I was banished, by treachery, to a life on the ocean—never again to be within sight of land, of green trees, golden beaches. I could still stir the wind and bring down lightning, but to what purpose? Destroy the ship I am on and myself along with it?

"Your Highness, luncheon is prepared."

"I'm not hungry," I said, hearing the sharpness in my voice as the server flinched back. They all feared me. Raising my power to defend my home turned all to strangers, even those who had known me from birth. Even my parents turned on me. They were the betrayers who had managed to get me on board this ship, unsuspecting of their intent.

The server may have flinched, but he was persistent. He knew, as they all did by now, that I would not actually harm them. I need them and am not so foolish to discard those that I need. He waited in silence to lead me to my midday meal. I bit back a sigh and turned away from the view of the endless sea and headed for the dining room where my entourage already waited. None were allowed to eat before I took my first bite. A foolish tradition, established by some long forgotten ancestor who apparently felt the need to force his pre-eminence down the throat of his subjects. No matter what I said now, I could not get anyone aboard this prison to discontinue that useless tradition.

They said this was a privilege, a luxury, an honor. That I was ambassador to all the kingdoms of the sea. An honored duty, one that a princess had never before been given. Not only was I tasked to represent my father's kingdom, but I was to find these mythical sea-people and forge an alliance with them. A pretty story to tell a confused child of only twelve years. At seventeen, the lie had worn thin. Five years since my foot had touched land. Five years since I had smelled fresh green things, moist dirt, walked through my father's palace. Five years since I had felt my mother's arms around me or heard my father's voice gently tease me.

Five long years to realize that my young instinct to protect my home had led to my banishment.

I entered the dining hall so luncheon could be served.

I woke from sleep with the moon still full and bright outside my window. Something had called me; I don't know what. My sleep was always deep and restful. Small noises never disturbed me, accustomed as I was to movement and voices surrounding me most of the time. I lay still, listening, waiting for whatever had roused me. My room was full of midnight shadow limned in silver. Moonlight reflected off of the mirrors and glass. My balcony doors were open, as usual.

It came again, a soft calling song. I pushed the light blanket off and stood up, pausing a moment to be sure of the call's direction. The balcony. The call came from the balcony. I waited no longer but stepped confidently towards this curious and unknown summons.

She leaned against the rail of my balcony, her back to me and face lifted to the moon above. Her hair was wet, hanging in long strands down her back. I could not determine the color under the moonlight, but it was dark. Her eyes, when she turned her head to look at me, were just as dark—inhuman, with no white to be seen. A complicated, twisting tattoo encircled her throat, the colors shimmering as she moved. Between her eyes, an oval of sea-opal reflected all the many colors of the oceans I had seen in the last five years.

She was not human. I was not afraid.

"Who are you to wake me from my sleep and summon me?" I asked, imbuing my voice with every bit of dignity and hauteur I had.

Her lips turned up as she spread a hand over the glistening ocean. "I am one of those you have been seeking. I am Liyana, of the house of Sidon, heir to the oceans and seas. We have watched you. We find you worthy."

I stepped closer. Worthy? The castoff daughter banished from land and home? Bitterness wanted to color my voice, but I had studied how to rule before my banishment, and one of those studies was on control of face and tone. These were tools to be used. "An honor, I have no doubt. It has been near half a decade that you have been watching. Why reveal yourself to me now?" My lips did not twist with cynicism. "What need do you have of me?"

Liyana laughed, the sound reminiscent of wind chimes: merry and bright. "We have no need of you. We have only a message to pass, one that we believe you have a right to know. We do not approve of what has been done with you. We do not like this land danger passed on to us who dwell within the deeps. You could turn your power to harm on us as easily as you could turn it to your enemies on land. You have not done so. You have done nothing that would lead us to think you would allow your power to run unchecked. So we come with a message: you must go home."

I laughed and lifted my arms. "This is my home. I have no other."

"Not so!" Liyana reached out and lowered my outspread arms. "You are of the land, and to the land you must go. We have long watched your kingdom, and we know of the danger it now faces. The forces that once threatened that home have massed again and are even now crossing our waters to threaten once more. You are needed."

"But not wanted." I turned away, and even all my control did not completely leech the bitterness from those words. Needed, perhaps. Not wanted, no longer. Once, I had been wanted, but not needed. I wished for those days again.

Liyana was silent a moment. "Sister," she said gently, "there is a price that comes with great power. As you are not asked if you wish for that power, you are not asked if you are willing to pay the price. These are not choices you have. The choice you have is whether that price will be a burden or a sacrifice freely given for love. It was your love that revealed your power to all and led to the price you paid, and continue to pay. But now you must choose: burden, or sacrifice? Will you leave your people to suffer, to be killed, and your land to be ravaged? You have the power to protect them, once again."

Her words burned me. Her gentleness shamed me. She was right. At twelve, I had not understood. At seventeen, I had the maturity and wit to understand the actions my parents had taken. I did not agree with them, but I knew fear for themselves alone would not have caused them to cast me away.

Burden or sacrifice? My choice must reflect the person I am, that I wish to be. Would I be a savior and once more earn banishment from my home? Or would I turn my back and let that which I had once prevented come to pass?

From the past, my father's voice echoed back to me. "We rule, but for the comforts and privileges we have, we can never put our wishes first. Our thoughts, our decisions, must always be for the good of the people who trust us to lead them. We are few; they are many. They are our children to protect and discipline, to guide and nurture. They must always come first, Ezrina. Always."

My people feared me, and to soothe them I was banished. But they were still my people, and there were some who had chosen banishment with me. They chose sacrifice. Could I do any less?

"Sister," Liyana said again and touched my cheek gently. "You always have a welcome home on the surface of the waters. Call your winds to fill your sails and make all speed."

The captain of the ship wanted to argue. I could sense that in him. His orders from his king were to keep me safely distant and to follow a regular course that brought the ship to ports on a regular basis—not that we ever docked. Tenders came and went, bringing supplies we needed, new staff. They did not know that the distance they kept from shore did not matter. If I could sense it, I could wield power. I chose not to. What purpose would it serve?

"Captain," I said, calmly, serenely, "you may turn this ship towards Atlantis. Or I will do so. Danger threatens our home, and I will not allow this."

"Your Highness, we are far from there. It will take weeks. Whatever threat there is will be well done and gone before we can come near."

I smiled reassuringly. "Not so, good captain. Turn this ship, and I will fill her sails with wind. We will fly over the waters, straight and true. Point the way, sir; it is time for us to go home."

The orders warred within him. King or princess? If the need did not exist, I would not put him in this position. My own young oaths bound me to obey my king, my father. Some things were more important. As I lifted my hand—an unnecessary gesture but a habit I had not yet broken—to stir the waters to carry the ship around, he sighed and rolled his shoulders.

"Turn the ship," he instructed his crew. "Head for capital port, Atlantis. Message the portmaster; we're coming home."

I smiled and laid my hand on the captain's shoulder. "Worry not, sir. The only harm that will come is to those who would threaten our home."

"And then, your Highness?" he asked doubtfully.

Indeed. What then?

I felt the fear of Atlantis before I could see her outline against the sky on the horizon. The unsettled prickle of wrong goose-bumped my skin. Perhaps it was my own emotions that I projected on my home.

I had thought much on what actions could be taken. I had spoken with my tutors and assessed the reasons for the last attack and the probable cause of the current one. Atlantis, land of wonder, magic, and beauty. No other land was as beautiful. No other country as advanced. Others were jealous of that beauty and the lives we lived. I knew what needed to be done, what only I could do. I could well guess the price I would pay.

Burden or sacrifice?

Ships unnumbered surrounded my home. Smoke rose from the port city. One of the palace towers was a crumbled ruin. Smoldering hulks floated on the water, dozens, burnt to the waterline, burning still inside. Small fishing boats searched for survivors, pulling them from the water and taking them ashore for tending.

Even as others sought to destroy Atlantis, her people still claimed they had no one they called enemy.

Saving these people would not change anything. Kindness and compassion only invited more attacks. The weapons my ancestors had built to protect us from this threat would not be used; I knew my father. He was a kind man, wise in his way. Life was precious, and he would not be the one to take any life.

Inside myself, I felt cold and distant. I reached for

my power. I sent out a call. Soon the sea boiled with the restless swarming of sharks. I raised my hands and once more called my power, raising the water high, higher, higher yet, towering over the ships. Down it came, controlled, slow enough to do no damage, hard and fast enough to sweep the decks clean. I needed the ships. I did not need the crews. The sharks fed and fed and fed as the waters shifted from clear turquoise and turned murky red. Distantly, I felt my stomach roil; my mind screamed. But again I raised the waters and brought them down. Some might survive. For the moment.

Ship by ship, I cleansed them of invaders. Guided them, unpopulated, into port. They floated there, serene and unthreatening. My people, small and almost indiscernible at this distant, came to inspect. They stopped and stared as my ship, my home, came into port and the crew cast lines to tie up on the royal dock. I stood in the prow alone, and watched as my people flinched back, huddled together, and whispered their fear as they saw me.

They feared me before. They feared me still. They would fear me more, but I would remove the danger from their lives.

A path opened and a cavalcade approached. My

father rode at the head, in full armor. I recognized him; he had changed little in five years, unlike myself. My child's body had matured into a young woman's. It took a moment for him to realize which ship this was and who stood waiting for him.

I felt cold. I needed to feel cold until this task was done.

My father did not wait for a groom to hold his stallion's bridle; he swung off the horse himself and left it untended as he rushed up the gangway that the crew had just slid out. His guards moved with him, swords half-drawn as their ward threw himself into reckless danger.

I waited for him to come to me. I could not be the daughter now, happy to see her father. There was work yet to be done. Before he reached me, arms already lifting to encircle me, I lifted my hand, palm out, and stop him with the smallest push of wind. I could *not* be his daughter now, or my resolve would waver and the actions I had already taken would be for nothing.

"They come out of jealousy, out of greed, for what we have and they do not. We are now what they will one day be, and they have not the patience to wait and

Burden or Sacrifice 13

work for that day. These attacks will not stop, and you will not do what must be done to stop them. The duty therefore falls to me.

"You, my father, my king, are a man of peace. You nurture and you grow. You are a good king, beloved by your people. But your strength is your weakness, and so I have but one choice: to do what must be done for the greater good or condemn my people to endless invasions until there is nothing left of them or of their home."

My father's eyes, so like my own, were soft with love, red with exhaustion, and lined with worry. I was wrong; he had changed much. He had aged although still a man in his prime. "Daughter, I have longed for the day I could see you again. I mourn that day comes at such a time. You have swept our attackers away, for I do not doubt that your will and power controlled the unnatural waves. Come, come home for the night, the week. See your mother, your sisters and brothers, and celebrate the end of this siege."

"I will not step foot on land," I said, now choosing the exile that had once been enforced on me. I understood, now, why it had to be done. My power would have brought more attacks, much earlier, than this. What I could do, what I controlled, inspired fear in others and that which is feared is destroyed. "Father, if peace is what you wish for your people, you must gather them together and find a new home for them. You and they must forsake the technology, knowledge, and magic that our people have amassed. Leave behind the weapons you will not use and luxuries that ease the tasks of life. Board these ships, sail away, and find peace in a distant land."

"Leave?" My king's eyes widened in shock. "Leave? This is our home! This is the place of our ancestors! How can we leave?"

I looked over the smoking city, the fallen tower. I heard the cries of those wounded, the wails of those holding their dead. "Can you stay and fight off more attacks? Can you stay and watch your people die?"

"Even if we leave, someone else will come and claim that which is ours as their own," my father objected.

"No," I answered. "None will come. I will see to that. But what must be done cannot be done while any that yet live remain on Atlantis." I paused, relented in the distance I kept from he who had once played with me in the gardens, tickled me until I was breathless with laughter, and guided my first adventures in exploring my power. I reached for his hands, lifted them to my heart. "Pray to the goddesses, Father, and they will answer. Go to mother and pray. Come tomorrow and tell me your answer. And remember: no living thing left behind, no part of Atlantis taken that is more than can be found in other lands."

I released his hands and stepped away. Back, back, back. I did not turn around. I allowed myself the indulgence of seeing him for as long as I could until bulkheads blocked my view.

When the choice was between his people and material things, I knew the choice my father would make. My heart remained cold. There would be time, and eternity, to mourn later.

Morning came, and with it the confused babble of people, the barnyard cacophony of animals. I stood on my balcony and watched as people herded their households aboard the ships waiting at harbor. Atlantis was a small country, the ships I had provided them would be enough and more to serve for the great evacuation. It was best I had not told my father my plan; he would never have allowed it. But he had prayed and the goddesses had answered. I took that as a blessing.

All day the ships loaded. As the sun sank, the

movement of people from land to ship trickled to a stop. Silence fell as the sun splashed crimson and gold over the sea. I reached with my senses, sweeping over my homeland, searching for living things that should not remain behind. Only small things, insects and worms, remained. All else that breathed and moved was gone, settling in on the ships that had come to destroy them. I released those ties and pushed the ships away, away, filling their sails with wind to send them free and clear of the work that must be done.

Once again, I lifted my hands to the sky. I sheathed my heart in ice again, thickening the shell. "This is my choice," I said to the waiting goddesses. "This is my duty. This is my sacrifice. I bear the burden from now until time ends."

I reached down, down, deep beneath the earth. I found the crack in the stone column that thrust Atlantis above the sea. I widened it, turning stone to pebbles, sweeping them aside. Once started, stone cracked and shifted on its own. More swiftly than I had intended, Atlantis started to sink. Water spread over the beaches slowly, then faster. The sea surged to fill the space the sinking land left open.

Down, down, down. My power guided my home.

Protected it from the damage the in-rushing sea would have caused. Down, down, down, the land of wonder went. Into the dark, into the deep. A thin barrier of air, set in place by my will, held there by the goddesses, protected Atlantis.

I was empty, depleted of all that I had. My head swam with exhaustion. As I sank to the deck of my ship, Liyana rose with the sea, and traded fins for legs as she went from water to ship. Her arms encircled me as the ice around my heart shattered. I wept, great heaving sobs that robbed my breath, deafened my ears, and weakened me even more.

"Sister, cry. Cry and mourn for the now, but know also that one day, you will raise Atlantis again. The sun shall shine and the flowers bloom on your home. Until that day, my kind will guard it from harm."

"I have sunk Atlantis, home of beauty and light. I have sunk Atlantis and banished myself forever from any home. My power is too great; wherever I go, those around me will not be safe."

"Burden or sacrifice, sister?" Liyana asked gently.

"Sacrifice," I answered without hesitation. "The choice was mine, knowing the outcome. I would choose so again."

Together we watched the sun rise to the east, spilling across the still, shining water where once my home stood. The ships of our enemies floated in the peaceful sea, but I could feel the grief and fear beating at me from every heart. Fear, fear of me. Hatred for me. Blame.

I would send the ships to safe harbor, on a land not so very far away. A land green and growing, much larger than Atlantis. They could take so little with them that they would have to begin anew. That which caused envy from others was gone. They would be safe. They would live.

And I would stay and guard Atlantis, until the time came for it to rise and its heirs to return.

Ameria Lewis has enjoyed indulging in literary escapism since she first learned to read. Writing was the next logical step. She has stories published in *Stepmothers and the Big Bad Wolf,* and *One Thousand Words for War.* When not working, writing, reading, or binge watching tv, she spends her time caring for her 4 cats and fostering kittens for a local cat rescue.

Daughter of Thorns

Hope Erica Schultz

If it had been a vid, it would have been a man that woke me.

Grandfather had called me Princess when he'd first shown me the pod and told me what I would have to do. "Our Sleeping Beauty, waiting for the right moment to wake." I'd wondered, then, who would find me, wake me, let my purpose unfold like a flower.

I was a little disappointed to see that it was a girl my age. Concern for me, a stranger, shone in her dark brown eyes. Not that I would have killed a man; allies are useful, and meat shields essential when you don't know what year it is.

And not that I wouldn't kill her, if I had to. But only if I had to.

"Don't be afraid," she whispered. The angels said that, in old stories, and parents to babies. Were the angels lying, too?

"Where…" That wasn't the question, of course, but it was a start. It gave less away than the real question.

"You're in New Washington, safe in a dome." She touched my wrist, glanced at a screen beside me. "I'm Sabi Mirza. I'm trained as a medic."

There hadn't been domes when I went under, nor a New Washington. "The others?" I asked, although I knew I'd been alone.

She shook her head, eyes bright with a sympathy I could use. "There was only you when we dug out the passage."

I sat carefully, allowing her to help me. It was better to look weak. "When is it?" I asked finally, the only important question. "What year is this?"

She hesitated a moment, and I met her gaze firmly. "2393," she answered at last.

I had been in cryo for over a hundred and fifty years.

She saw the shock on my face, and I let her hold me as I cried. It wasn't feigned, none of it was. Oh, everyone I'd ever loved had already been dead when I went into that tube, but it had been over a century and a half.

Now the people who had killed them were dead, too.

"My name is Rose," I said when she brought me clothes, took me to a shower that had actual warm water. "Rose Elizabeth Dorn." There was no sense in lying about that. They ought to be able to learn my name with a simple retinal scan, and lying about it would make them distrust me.

Sabi didn't make any noises about finding my family, which was comforting. Even if any had survived—and I knew they hadn't—their descendants would be as much strangers as she was.

When I was clean and dressed in fresh clothes—a tunic and leggings in crimson and gold—I paused to study my rescuer. She was shorter than me, a little, with slanted eyes, brown skin, curly black hair. No particular ethnicity that I could detect. I wondered if everyone was indistinct in this century, if my blond hair and blue eyes would make me memorable.

Memorable is bad.

She smiled and gestured towards a hallway. "The others are waiting for you. It is supper time." She walked beside me but did not touch me. "I am sorry; this will all seem strange to you. My greater-family has claim to this dome and the rubble beneath it. That you were found here means you are family-by-right and have a claim on our hospitality if you choose." She looked at me earnestly. "You really must, until you are strong again. If there is elsewhere you wish to go, we will manage a dowry for you."

I hid my expression behind one hand, as if overwhelmed, and nodded.

The hall opened into a large room with multiple tables. I counted nineteen adults, five children, and the two of us as we entered. Weapons were scarce—cooking knives, glassware that could be broken, pottery that could be thrown. One other exit at the far end looked unguarded.

A tall man stood and bowed to me as I approached. "I am Mirza Hasan, first shareholder in this family. We welcome you into our home." His brown eyes were like Sabi's and just as kind. I smiled tremulously and glanced around the room. Not a single angry or suspicious face. If the gods had actually existed, I would have thought they had finally decided to favor me.

"Your kindness soothes my grief," I murmured, something my grandmother had taught me, before. *Show appreciation, but always remind them that you are deserving of their pity.* From their expressions, it was successful on both counts.

"Come, sit, and eat. You are welcome here," Mirza Hasan said gently, and I nodded, and sat.

Sabi tried to explain the Fall to me, but she had duties. To my secret delight she logged me in to a computer system to search out the answers for myself. There were a few articles looking back, but the most useful things I found were vids for small children, explaining history. There had been wars, a few, and diseases, more than a few, but what had finally crushed humanity down to the domes was both simpler and more complex.

Babies weren't being born.

In the domes, one out of every four to six pregnancies resulted in a live birth. Outside of them, essentially none. There were a lot of things in the atmosphere to account for it, but it wasn't just one, or just two, or just a dozen. There were literally hundreds of chemicals outside, impacting this.

The entire population of the world was down to a few million people.

The records of my family were surprisingly intact. We were painted as the villains, as the losers of a war generally are. The rival family who had destroyed us, however, were eventually considered our murderers. Some few even went to prison. I stared at their pictures a long time, longer than at the pictures of my dead relatives.

If our enemies had children, grandchildren … it would be great-grandchildren at least, with no memory of the generation who had turned my life into hell. There might be some justice in killing them, but there wouldn't be any satisfaction. They wouldn't know why. That, grandfather always said, was a waste of a kill.

I turned the computer off and stared at the ceiling, wondering what purpose I could find here.

We went to the city a few days later.

I had had a fairly isolated childhood, but the city still seemed ridiculously small, a dome of a few thousand people. Sabi and her family traded materials they had reclaimed from beneath their dome for food and cloth and other necessities, while some among them traded labor for less well-defined things—utilities?

I helped Sabi carry a crate of materials from the truck, an enclosed vehicle that looked like a cross between an old-fashioned minivan and a futuristic tank. She knew everyone we encountered, which would have been strange in the cities I had visited in the past. She introduced me to everyone, and I smiled and nodded and pretended not to follow the names.

The town had expanded downward, under the

dome, and there was a warren of passage-ways below the surface. I helped her lug the crate through them, commenting on how impossible it was to know which was which while I carefully cataloged every turn and marking. Good humored incompetence, my grandfather always said, left people too self-satisfied to distrust you.

Sabi smiled and chatted with everyone we met until we actually delivered the crate. Her chatter dried up, and her smile went flat, and she just nodded to the man working in the little factory room.

"Mr. Anders."

"Miss Mirza." He nodded back, a skinny man, pale as me, with tufts of brown hair and haunted eyes. There was a band across his forehead, metallic, looking like it was fused with his flesh or maybe with the bone beneath. He looked at me, caged wolf to free, and looked away.

"We can leave them here, Rose. Mr. Anders will take care of them." She seemed anxious to get away, and I followed her, remapping the path in my mind to make sure I had it memorized.

She paused after a bit. "Mr. Anders is one of the altered. He was broken, and he—he hurt someone. He's fixed now, so he won't hurt anyone else."

I processed that a moment. "The band on his forehead?"

Sabi nodded. "They were invented soon after you—a long time ago."

I nodded back, my mind working on possibilities.

There were seventeen altered in the New Washington Dome. Twelve were for repeated theft or simple assaults, and I ignored them. Two were for rape, two more for the murder of an adult … and Sabi's Mr. Anders was for the murder of a child. Aaila Mirza, a four-year-old who must have been Sabi's baby sister.

The device claimed to remove the desire to commit the crime rather than volition or intelligence. I doubted that. Lack of desire wouldn't have made Anders twitch like a caged beast.

I switched the computer to other matters, reluctant to leave too much of a trail. I wasn't going to get to avenge my family; it seemed only right that I instead avenge the family who had taken me in.

I was blessed with wide eyes, short stature, a soft voice. People trusted me easily, liked the way I made fun of myself for my poor sense of direction. Sabi's family was already popular, and these people accepted me as one of them. It was almost too easy.

I didn't dare go after Ander's first, with his connection to Sabi's family. Instead I picked the woman who had strangled her neighbor over a fight about radishes. I could not imagine anyone killing for radishes, but as I was only killing her as a cover, I didn't feel that I should judge. She was guilty, and that was more than enough.

The market day I proved that I could (slowly and laboriously) follow the route between greenhouse and the dome's gate on my own, I was finally left alone with an errand I could do in a quarter of the time expected. A quick detour to the canning room where the woman worked alone, a quick twist of wire, and I had plenty of time to bring my supplies (including the now clean wire) to the greenhouse and return with fresh vegetables to the gate. Her body hadn't even been discovered when we left for home.

I was startled to see Sabi crying about the death the next morning. "Was she a friend of yours?" I asked, mildly perturbed.

Sabi shook her head. "I doubt if she had any friends. But she was alive, and now she's not. We're one life closer to extinction."

Soft hearted sheep are frequently incomprehensible. I patted her arm and said nothing.

I waited a few weeks for the next target, a man who had beaten another man to death with a crowbar. He, too, seemed friendless. He, too, worked alone, sheering sheep. I brought him a drink of water, bashed his head in with the hilt of a sheering knife when he turned away, and then carefully cut his throat into the barrel he was using to wash the fleece. Wiping prints, I resumed my supposed path to a completely different part of the dome, being sure to stop and ask for directions in the area furthest from the sheering pen.

There was an even greater distress over this death, which irked me mildly. If you choose to be sheep and not defend yourself against the wolves, why do you get so upset if someone else steps up to do so?

I was, though, looking forward to Ander's death. He had wronged Sabi's family as surely as the rival family that killed mine had wronged me. I considered a thousand ways to kill him, discarding one after another—too melodramatic. Too painless. Too quick. Too messy.

I waited for a trip where no one in the family had anything to bring to him, nothing to tie us to the vicinity. My poor sense of direction was still the subject of much

Daughter of Thorns

good-natured teasing, but I was being allowed more and more on my own. It was easy to slip below to the tunnels, to follow that path, a 'borrowed' pruning knife in one hand. I turned the final corner ... and stopped. Sabi was waiting outside his door.

"You can't do this, Rose."

There was such quiet sorrow in her voice that I stopped. "He killed your sister," I said, not even pretending to misunderstand.

She nodded. "He was broken, and he killed her. Killing him won't bring her back ... it only removes one more life from the world. We're so close to extinction. 'Save one life, save the world.'" She reached out a hand to me. "Your heart is good, Rose. We can help you. You don't have to do this anymore."

I could gut her in seconds, knock out Anders, hang him like a suicide with the knife in his hand. It was the sensible thing to do.

"You think I'm broken," I said instead, surprised at the hurt in my own voice.

"We can help you," she repeated. "You don't have to be a killer. You can be who you were meant to be."

I smiled, the knife cool in my hand. Two steps, thrust in and up. "You think the violence is like a tumor in me, Sabi, something that can be cut out. It isn't. It's what I am. It's what I was born for."

I raised the knife, held her eyes with my own. "You don't understand, and you never will. You choose to stay a sheep in this pasture you've made for yourself, neutering the wolves when they appear. I can't save you from that, Sabi. But I'm going to give you a gift. I'm going to give you your life."

I heard her sudden cry, but the knife was already turning in my hand. Cold as fire, it bit into my throat.

Hope Erica Schultz writes science fiction and fantasy stories for kids, teens, and adults. Her first novel, the young adult post-apocalyptic *Last Road Home*, came out in 2015, and she co-edited of the YA anthology *One Thousand Words for War*. Her stories have appeared in multiple anthologies and magazines.

Cold Bargain

Jeanne Kramer-Smyth

A soft rustle pulled Cress's gaze up to the moonlit sky. A large shape hurtled down, a dark smudge against the moon-silvered branches. Cress braced her feet on the uneven frozen path and drew her sword. She cut the creature out of the air before it could peck out her eyes, rending head from body, and stepped aside to avoid most of the gore. The crow's feathers and blood painted the snow black.

One feather shifted. Cress felt no breeze against her face, yet the feather flipped and spun. She stepped back, raising her sword. More feathers were moving now, dancing back to the crow's body. Dark blood streamed back into its neck. Its head and body reconnected like some strange child's toy with detachable pieces. The creature hopped onto its feet, feathers smoothed back in place, and looked at her.

She didn't wait to see if it would attack her again. Cress took one beat to get her bearings, sheathed her sword and raced along the path. Running uphill, weaving through thick undergrowth and between wide tree trunks, she put one foot ahead of the other until she could barely breathe. She stumbled into a small clearing. This had to be the one she had been hunting for.

Cress's cheeks burned from the cold. Her eyes watered. She turned to watch the path behind her, but she could make out nothing pursuing her through the gloom.

She walked to the center of the clearing. The ground lay bare, but the night air still blew cold. It smelled like snow and fir trees. Dozens of tree trunks reached toward the sky, the high evergreens' branches framing the full moon.

Something shifted overhead. Cress held her breath. Wings. Silent birds hiding in the shadows.

Turning slowly, Cress watched the treetops. The wind died down, yet the trees' edges still moved. First one bird rose into the sky and then another. She squared her shoulders and readied her sword, but they only circled and settled back into the tree line. A moment later, three more birds did the same.

She had found the roost. The crow she had tried to kill, likely guarding the perimeter, had not yet raised the alarm.

Cold Bargain   33

Cress wiped her watering eyes and dripping nose. Barely a dry spot remained on her jacket sleeve. She closed her eyes and breathed into the fabric. It still smelled faintly of home, of the herbs that her mother often sprinkled on the fire to soothe her grandmother's labored breathing.

Cress stepped to the edge of the clearing and swung her pack from her back so it landed neatly at her feet. Kneeling on the frigid ground, she fumbled the cold metal latches open and wrestled out a large wrapped bundle. She gently unraveled the fabric until she held the still body of a sleek black crow. Cress cradled the bird in her left arm and walked back to the center of the space. She pulled a small pouch from her belt and stamped her tingling feet against the cold. Had it been like this when her grandmother had come here? Had she been alone in the woods in the middle of the night—a dead bird in one hand and pouch of salt in the other? Cress blew out a long cloudy breath.

Grandmother's journal stayed stashed away. Cress had memorized the summoning ritual hidden in its coded pages. The salt made a neat white line as she poured it out to mark a circle about four feet across. At the circle's center she set the crow, then carefully stepped back over the line.

Almost immediately, a whooshing sound drew her eyes back to the sky. A cloud of black avian bodies swarmed down and along the edges of the clearing.

The dark whirlwind surrounded both Cress and the white salt circle, the sound of the wings deafening. The black whirl grew denser as more birds flew down from the trees.

Cress stood her ground. She watched the bird she had left in the circle until a pillar of black mist formed above it and obscured her view.

From the center of the dark cloud came a woman's voice singing, clear and high. Cress didn't understand the words, but the tone was joyful. The song became stronger, exultant, weaving through the clearing and rising up into the trees. Surely this had to be magic, for now Cress's face stopped burning and muscles she hadn't realized were braced against the cold began to relax as the clearing grew warm. The song ended and the crows that had encircled her streamed silently back to their roost.

A spark of light flickered in the center of the circle's mist. The glow grew in intensity until the swirling mass dissipated to reveal a woman clad in white. She held a tall torch, like a flaming spear.

Ornate tattoos covered her face, dark blue against her milky skin. Long hair, the color of the last embers of a fire. The palest eyes Cress had ever seen, the shade of a stormy sky just past dawn. Her white gown, crafted of gossamer fabric, stretched to the ground but left her arms bare. The tattoos continued down her arms in long abstract lines. They were not quite vines, but more like the paths water can carve in a steep hillside.

Was there any stretch of her skin not tattooed? Cress tried to imagine what designs like that would look like on her own dark skin. A dark enough pigment could be quite striking.

The Sorceress released her grasp on the torch. It stood tall, without support, on the stone hard ground beside the crow's body.

"Who has summoned me and disturbed my rest? Come into the light, let me see you." The Sorceress waved her forward. "Do I know you?" she asked. Cress stepped fully into the torch's light, hand on the sword at her waist. She fought not to reveal her anxiety, to breathe the warm air evenly. The white-clad woman stalked slowly forward across the line of salt, but stayed out of Cress's sword range. She looked Cress over carefully before answering her own question with a quick shake of her head. "I think not."

Cress eyed the path away from the clearing, but grandmother had no one else to do this for her. The Sorceress was her only chance. Cress's rehearsed words froze in her throat. She hadn't spoken to another person in weeks. Had she forgotten how?

"My name is Cress," she choked out, then cleared her throat and continued, "Please forgive me, but I disturb your rest with good reason." She stepped forward, holding out her hand. It only trembled a little.

"Oh." The Sorceress seemed a bit startled. "Yes. Very well. My name is Mata-Linda." She stepped forward again and took Cress's dark hand in her pale one. She turned their joined hands from side to side for a moment, then let go. She returned her gaze to Cress's face. "Who has sent you? What do they want of me?"

"I have come of my own choice. I return to you one of your own."

Mata-Linda looked down to where Cress gestured. She crumpled to her knees with a quiet gasp, gathering up the bird and folding its rigid body to her chest. Mata-Linda closed her eyes and murmured quietly, rocking the creature back and forth.

"I found the bird already dead on the floor of my

grandmother's bedroom," Cress added quietly. "I seek a release for her from your enchantment."

"You come to have me undo something?" Mata-Linda looked up at her, tilting her head, still clutching the bird close. "I am much more of a doer than an un-doer."

"You cursed my grandmother, Queen Frederica." Cress bit out. "She who once received foreign dignitaries clad in a gown the color of the brightest poppies. Do you even remember her?"

"Cursed? I am not in the habit of cursing people. Messy business, curses." She shook her head as if trying to get a bad taste out of her mouth.

"She has not eaten for months, yet she will not die. She is an empty shell of the woman she used to be." Her grandmother's journal had led Cress to find the crows' roost and the Sorceress. It told nothing of how to undo the curse, but the common wisdom agreed that a Sorceress's curses would fall away if she died. "What is to stop me from killing you and undoing all your magic?"

"This." Mata-Linda made no gesture from where she knelt on the ground, but suddenly Cress could no longer move. She could take shallow breaths, but no more, until the Sorceress released her. "Right. So no trying to cut off my head."

"Uh huh." Cress coughed, nodding.

"Are you are done attempting to kill me?"

Cress quickly nodded again.

Mata-Linda glared at her once more before shifting to gently lay the black bird back on the ground at the center of the circle. She began a new song, melancholy and complex. Cress still understood none of the words, but the sentiment carried through. It brought new tears to her eyes, from emotion rather than cold. Mata-Linda's hands began to glow a bright white. A strong smell, of fruit and spices, almost overwhelmed Cress.

The sorceress slowly brought her hands down to the bird's body. The bird's feathers absorbed the glow until the entire body of the bird cast a silvery white light. Mata-Linda's voice reached a crescendo and the light grew so bright that Cress had to look away. When she could look back, the light had faded. In its place, a live black crow hopped from foot to foot, glossy feathers reflecting the moonlight.

"What does this bird have to do with my Grandmother?" Cress asked.

"She never explained to you what she had become?"

"Become?"

"I remember your grandmother." Mata-Linda stood slowly. "Frederica paid me well to cast that enchantment. She was sick when she came to me, with young children and a kingdom depending on her." Mata-Linda looked her up and down. She stepped to stand in front of Cress, but did nothing magical to hold her in place. "Hold still please." She put her hand on Cress's cheek and hummed softly. Cress's face vibrated gently and grew warm. The air around her head smelled of cinnamon as Mata-Linda closed her eyes and stood that way for an endless minute. When her hand fell away, Cress's skin felt cold where the hand had been. "*You* are healthy."

"You can tell?"

"It is one of my skills." Mata-Linda tipped her head in agreement as she stepped back, still watching her intently. "What are *your* skills?"

"My grandmother made sure I trained in the sword." Cress laid a hand on sword at her waist. "Shall I show you?"

Mata-Linda nodded once, clearing the way for Cress to demonstrate.

Cress took off her gloves and unwrapped the scarf from around her head, tucking them into her belt. She went into her favorite practice sequence. Awkward beneath the heavy winter layers, she still moved through the full set. The sword whistled through the air—the blade's balance familiar and comforting. The cousins had always mocked her obsession with the sword, but her grandmother had always been proud of her dedication.

When she finished, returning the blade to its sheath, Mata-Linda smiled at her, her eyes bright and thoughtful.

"Yes, you are quite fine indeed. And your grandmother also shared with you her wisdom as a ruler?"

"I suppose. She liked having me nearby. No one really notices a girl in the shadows." Cress shrugged. "You still haven't told me what you did to her."

"I did not." She sighed, then nodded to herself. "To heal her I transformed her. I shared with her my power to transform into birds. In exchange, your grandmother vowed to protect a vulnerable border of my land." The sorceress glanced at the moon now beginning to slip behind the tree branches. "She had to shift every month on the night of the full moon into a murder of crows. But she was much older than I was when I became what I am. And death can only be warded off for so long." Mata-Linda turned back to her. "Have you been finding the dead birds frequently?"

"Yes." The crow now hopped around on the ground at Mata-Linda's feet. "When I found my grandmother's journal I realized they might have something to do with her sickness. Can you save her? Or release her?"

"I cannot save her." Mata-Linda looked sad. Resigned. "I will release Queen Frederica if you pledge to serve me in her place."

"Serve you?" Cress asked.

"You are trained in combat. You fought my scout and survived my lands in deep winter. And you found a way to call me from my winter roost." The crow flew up to sit on Mata-Linda's shoulder. She absent-mindedly reached to smooth its feathers. "My woods are extensive and the villages that are loyal to me need protection. She who breached my defenses seems the best candidate to reinforce them. With your grandmother released from my service, my lands will lose one of their best defenders."

"How long must I serve you?"

"For as long as your grandmother's enchantment lasted."

"And if I do not survive long enough?"

"Then you will have paid the price for her release

with what remains of your life."

Cress considered leaving—walking out of the freezing forest and returning home. She doubted that Mata-Linda would stop her. The kingdom would survive her power hungry uncles or it would not. But it was the thought of returning to see her grandmother still a breathing husk of a woman, the thought of finding those dead crows month after month, year after year, that convinced her. "I say yes, and you will set her free?"

"We will need something a bit more binding than just your word." The crow cawed in agreement. "But first, *do* you agree?" Mata-Linda waited. The crow shifted, watching Cress with its black eyes.

"Yes." Cress spat it out quickly, before she could change her mind. Cress's heart raced, but she stayed still.

Mata-Linda gave her no time to reconsider. She walked quickly forward and took Cress's face in both her hands. The scent of cinnamon returned. The first time the Sorceress touched her, only her face had warmed, but now her entire body grew hot. It quickly became almost unbearable, her skin feeling as if it crawled with fire ants. She grabbed Mata-Linda's wrists, pulling on them to break free, to make the burning stop. The

Sorceress was strong or her magic made the connection unbreakable.

"Stop fighting," Mata-Linda whispered. Her tattoos shifted across her skin. "Let go and let me in." Cress took a deep breath and closed her eyes. She pictured her grandmother's smiling face, imagined her warm loving arms holding her close. The crawling on her skin faded. The heat moved deeper within her, like the warmth from a hearty stew on a cold day. Cress relaxed and let Mata-Linda work. When she opened her eyes, the world appeared different—brighter and warmer. "When I need you at my side, you will feel the pull to return to your sword." Cress tightened her grip on it. Mata-Linda smiled. "But now, go say goodbye to your dear grandmother." Mata-Linda waved her hand and Cress felt herself begin to fall away. She panicked as the world divided. Cress looked out of many sets of eyes. She flew up into the treetops, struggling to control all the winged bodies she suddenly inhabited. Starlings. Hundreds of starlings whirling through the branches in the moonlight.

Her grandmother taught her to call a group of starlings a murmuration. They had been one of Frederica's favorite birds, wheeling around the castle towers at sunset each day.

The starlings cleared the treetops, turning as one to fly south. Perhaps every murmuration was a person like herself, one mind controlling all the birds at once. The land it had taken Cress nearly a month to cross as a human, took less than a day for the murmuration. She marveled at the speed of their flight, at the beauty of the lands unfolding beneath her. As she reached her grandmother's castle at sunset the next day, the death bells were already ringing. The starlings swarmed through the open windows of Frederica's chambers, filling the room with wings and cries.

The family stood at the queen's bedside as her chief advisor unsealed Frederica's succession decree. Cress tried to transform into her human form again, but Mata-Linda's magic wouldn't permit it. Her mother and uncles and brothers shrieked and swatted at her, racing from the room. The advisor dropped the scroll, abandoning it open on the floor.

Cress stared at her name on the parchment in her grandmother's tight script. Through all her starling eyes she saw it over and over. She appreciated that Frederica wanted that for her. Cress would have been the youngest queen in the kingdom's long history. But she had made her choice to set Frederica free, and she couldn't turn back now.

The queen lay wrapped in a fine linen shroud. Cress spread the starlings out across its length, grabbing tightly with their tiny claws. More starlings reached for the edges of the sheet beneath the queen. They adjusted and shifted until, flapping their wings, they lifted her. The murmuration carried the queen's body off into the darkening sky.

Jeanne Kramer-Smyth has been writing stories since she first got her hands on a typewriter when she was 9. A fan of many types of fiction, she has a special place in her heart (and large home library) for fantasy, science-fiction, YA, and historical fiction. She is currently an archivist by day and a writer, glass artist, and fan of board games by night. She lives in Maryland with her husband, son, sister-in-law, and cat. Visit her at http://www.jeannekramersmyth.com.

A Princess, a Mission, and a Kiss

Lori Bond

"Presenting Her Serene Highness, Princess Isabelle of Neubaden."

Isabelle paused for a moment at the top of the grand staircase leading down into the New Year's Ball being held at the Vieux Palais in Brussels. She gave the paparazzi ranged on either side of the landing a dazzling smile, the one the London tabloids called "diabolically charming."

While the Herald announced her father, the Prince of Neubaden, and his latest wife, Isabelle moved down the steps and into the party. She paused in her slow meandering around the room to take selfies with the French Prime Minister and the Colsteinburg Ambassador to the EU. She joined various conversations and made the same comment about the amazing decorations over and over as if she were as vapid as her blonde hair implied. If she were being honest, she didn't think much of the decorations beyond the cover they gave the hidden Belgian snipers guarding all of the visiting royalty and dignitaries at the event. But, the socialite she played in real life wouldn't have noticed, so Isabelle didn't comment either. Instead she continued to circle the event, making small talk and posting meaningless updates on social media. She snagged a glass of champagne she wouldn't be old enough to legally drink for years and kept one eye out for her target.

Constantin looked up from his phone when they announced Isabelle of Neubaden. He just barely managed not to snort that she had been called "serene." He knew that this was the traditional way the German princes and their families styled themselves, but he'd never heard of anyone less serene than Isabelle.

"Isn't that the girl Father wants you to meet?" asked his older brother. Pieter was the golden boy of the Corvin family—handsome, smart, and the natural to follow their father in his food import and export business once Pieter left Cambridge next term. There was only one thing Constantin had ever managed to do that Pieter hadn't done first and better. Constantin had been accepted to L'École Suisse, the elite boarding school where the richest and most powerful people sent their children. Once Constantin started school he'd be sharing a three room suite with a Saudi prince and an heir to the second wealthiest oligarch in Russia, but to cement his social standing at the school—and the future business opportunities they would represent—he needed to get in good with the school's reigning princess. Isabelle of Neubaden might be from an outdated principality with no real political power, but her social capital bought more friends than all the gold in the vault under the New York Federal Reserve.

"Isn't she?" Pieter prompted.

"Isn't she what?"

"Focus." Pieter acted like he was going to snatch the phone out of Constantin's hand, but they both knew it was a feint. "Isn't Isabelle the girl Father wants you to chat up?"

Constantin nodded but didn't speak. His eyes raked the crowd searching for the golden haired girl in the excessively daring designer dress.

Pieter shoved him from behind. "Get going then. You don't want to disappoint Father." Pieter said this as if were the worst threat he could envision.

Constantin tried not to roll his eyes. To Pieter, who had never disappointed their father, at least not in living memory, there probably wasn't a worse fate. For Constantin who had been nothing but a disappointment since birth (as if he could control that he hadn't been the much desired girl), disappointing his father just meant it was Tuesday.

He finally spotted the princess laughing with a minor adjunct from his country's embassy. Constantin smiled a smile that was more like a predator baring his teeth than a reflection of his mood.

Isabelle pretended to give the Hungarian spy her full attention while he said vaguely sexist remarks about the shape of her dress. The real Isabelle would have made a cutting comment about his manhood or lack thereof, but the real Isabelle had been tucked away three years ago when she agreed to join the youth division of the German spy organization, the BND. With her mother's tech money and her father's connections as Europe's number one unrepentant playboy, she had been uniquely situated to infiltrate the highest levels of society, levels the average BND-J could only dream of achieving. Most of the time she made headlines and provided distractions when important BND operations needed cover. Trading on her Father's dissolute reputation, she had crafted her own party girl image with the help of some carefully timed BND sponsored posts.

She made another inane comment to the spy, certain he was paying as little attention to her as she was to him. Without appearing to break eye contact, she scanned the crowd directly behind the man. There had been no sign of the target, but one of his sons, the younger one, seemed to be headed for her. He had the single focused stare that teenaged boys got when they were on a mission. For a second she wondered if her assignment had been blown, if the kid had been sent as an intercept to keep her away from his father. Then he caught her staring and smiled. Her gut clenched, but she smiled back, her mind spinning with possibilities and alternate plans. Her own mission might have just gotten infinitely more pleasant.

"Hi, I'm Constantin." Constantin interrupted the conversation with no style and even less grace. The diplomat from the Embassy raised an eyebrow but didn't comment on Constantin's rudeness. It was one of the few benefits of being a Corvin. It didn't make up for his father's soul-crushing expectations, but it was a benefit.

A Princess, a Mission, and a Kiss 51

Constantin turned to the breathtaking girl beside the embassy flunkie. Up close, she was better looking than the paparazzi shots he'd seen online. Her face was animated with an intelligence the vultures of the press had never managed to capture in their quest to add to her reputation as a party girl drinking her way through Europe. "You're Princess Isabelle, right?"

The princess nodded. "Most people just call me Isabelle though." She leaned in as if sharing a daring secret, her hand resting lightly on his jacket sleeve for just a moment. Constantin's arm felt like it had caught on fire. He didn't hiss in surprise, but it was a near thing. "Royalty is so last century, don't you think?" She spoke so low, she practically whispered in his ear. Her breath brushed his face like the gentlest of breezes.

Constantin's jaw dropped, and he stuttered out something in response.

Isabelle smiled again. Constantin was cute in an adorable I Have No Idea How to Talk to Girls kind of way. Considering how hot he was, and he was yummy in his tuxedo, she was surprised he wasn't a better flirt. Most guys in her world were players, jumping from one conquest to the next as soon as they turned fourteen. She knew from his dossier that Constantin was a year older than her, seventeen, but he was blushing like a kid holding a girl's hand for the first time. It was refreshing. It was sweet. It was distracting her from her mission.

She pulled herself back into the game. Using every technique drilled into her from her Langley tutor, she put Constantin at ease and got him talking about himself. She found a sweet, well-meaning boy hiding beneath someone attempting to be cynical and all-knowing. Without him realizing, she even got him to admit that he only talked to her because his father wanted him to make only the best connections once he started her school. The more Constantin spoke about his hideous father, the more resolved she became to successfully complete her mission. According to their intel, the older brother Pieter was a mirror image of the gun-running head of the Corvin family, both in looks and spiteful temperament, especially towards enemies. How that man had raised an innocent like Constantin was beyond her.

Constantin had never felt so comfortable with another person in his entire life. He had no real friends back home since his father deemed very few people worthy of associating with a Corvin. His father's business associates and their kids found him lacking the traits they valued most—greed, ruthlessness, and a complete disregard for other people and their feelings. Constantin had coped by speaking as little as possible with a cynical outlook on the rare occasion he was forced to socialize. It had been a lonely and isolating experience, and being so open with Isabelle only highlighted how stifling his own life had been.

"It's nearing midnight," he said to Isabelle, unable to keep the regret out of his voice. This had been the best hour of his life, but he knew he couldn't monopolize her all evening.

"So?" She gave him another one of those dazzling smiles, one that made him glad he had already leaned against one of the pillars lining the room, otherwise he might have fallen down. "It's not like I'm going to turn into a pumpkin at midnight." Her smile turned mischievous. "Are you?"

Constantin sputtered. "No, of course not," he managed to get out. "It's just midnight, New Year's Eve." His voice trailed off, and the blood rushed to his cheeks.

They had been watching the dancers twirl around

the center of the room, but now Isabelle turned to give Constantin her full attention. "Why, Mr. Corvin," she said in English, in an excellent imitation of an American woman from one of the old movies about their Civil War, "are you angling for a kiss?"

If his face had been flushed before, it must be fire engine red now. His mouth moved, but no sounds came out. He probably looked like a drowning fish.

"Because if that is what you're thinking," Isabelle said, switching back to the German they'd been speaking all night, "I think it's a very good idea."

Constantin tried to swallow, but he had trouble getting anything past the huge lump in his throat. His heart was beating so fast, he thought it might fall out of his chest and go racing around the room. "Oh, okay," he said. The blood seemed to be leaving his head, shooting to other, more embarrassing places. He both wanted to kiss her and wanted the Earth to open up and swallow him whole.

"However, I do not kiss and tell," Isabelle said, glaring for a moment at the line of photographers along the upper railings shooting at the glittering crowd below. When he must have looked a bit puzzled, she added in a dark tone, "Not when it matters."

"Oh."

Neither of them said anything else for a moment. They grinned at one another, but these weren't the smiles that they used for the public, the ones for the cameras or for his father. These were small, intimate smiles, ones that confirmed that for now, only the two of them mattered.

"Let's go then," said Constantin. Taking a deep breath, he did the bravest thing of his life. He reached over and grabbed her hand.

Isabelle let Constantin lead her out of the ballroom into a service hallway behind the main rooms.

"Do you think we're safe here?" he asked.

She laughed at his innocence, the sound filled with more humor than she felt. Even if she hadn't been a trained spy, she would have known better than to kiss in the hallway of a public building, no matter how deserted the corridor might appear. She pointed up at the cameras mounted along the upper reaches of the walls. "You'd be surprised what an underpaid security guard will sell to the press."

Constantin looked thoughtful. "You would know better than me. Where do you suggest we go? I've never had to worry much about the press. My father doesn't really crave publicity."

Well, most gun-running international criminals are not big on PR, Isabelle wanted to say, but she physically bit her tongue instead. The sharp pain reminded her to stay on task. Her goal was to get in the Corvin's suite and copy the gun-runner's hard drive, not make the man's younger son into her new best friend with benefits. She needed Constantin to take her to his room and for it to be his own idea.

"There must be someplace we can go with no cameras, and maybe a door." Isabelle paused for a second, but Constantin didn't seem to be getting the hint. "If only we were staying here at the Palais, but Papa isn't welcome most places anymore, not with the way he trashes hotels with his all-night parties. We've had to put up with family friends." She hoped she wasn't laying it on too thick.

"Oh, of course," Constantin said, finally catching on. "I don't know why I didn't think of it right off. We're actually staying here in one of the suites. There's a whole contingent of diplomats, businessmen, and other important people staying in one of the wings."

In anyone else, Isabelle would have assumed that last bit was a dig to remind her that the German princes weren't quite the important people they had once been during the Austro-Hungarian empire, but from Constantin's eager tone and open face, she knew he meant nothing by it. Her heart pinched a little bit at the deception she was playing on him. She swore to herself that when they both got to school in three weeks, she would watch out for him, both as penance and because she didn't want this lovely soul eaten alive by the brats at her school.

Constantin took them to his family's suite, only getting lost once on the way. Isabelle had the entire building's floor plan memorized, including all the duct work, service corridors, and any other escape route, but she couldn't tell Constantin that. She couldn't let him know that she knew the exact position to his suite and twelve different routes between it and the ballroom.

After what felt like an eternity, they turned the final corner and nearly ran straight into the two security goons guarding the door. These weren't the rent-a-cops used by the Palais and other museums around Brussels. These were a pair of gun-toting, burly guards ready to take down any threat to the Corvins. Isabelle giggled and hid her head on Constantin's shoulder like she was embarrassed. Really, she wanted to scope out the guards without them getting a clear look at her face. Finding the man and woman in front of the doors wasn't a surprise, but they were an unwelcome development.

"Uh, hi," said Constantin. He walked past the two stone-faced guards. Neither said a word although the man reached over and opened the door for them. They passed through, and finally, Isabelle was in the target's suite. Her eyes darted around the room searching for the gun-runner's laptop.

Finally, Constantin had gotten Isabelle back to his family's rooms. He hoped she hadn't noticed that it took them so long because he got lost. She hadn't said anything, so if she had noticed, she'd been nice enough not to embarrass him about it.

"Have you ever been in one of the private suites before?" he asked her.

"No," she stopped looking around and gave him a half-smile. "Is it that obvious?"

"You seem to be taking in everything at once."

Isabelle looked a little disconcerted for a moment, like it bothered her that he'd noticed her staring. The place was hard not to stare at though. It had been built, and decorated, during the Baroque period, and everything was a bit over the top. There were modern hints like the mini-fridge in the wardrobe, but the uncomfortable chairs and velvet wallpaper made it hard to look away when you first walked in.

"It's certainly something," Isabelle said. She turned and stood a little closer to Constantin. "It's almost midnight," she whispered. Her breath once again tickled his cheek.

He didn't take a step back although his heart had stopped for a moment and then restarted at a speed that just might kill him. He glanced at the delicate clock sitting on the mantle. "Just a few more seconds," he whispered back, afraid his voice would do something mortifying like crack if he tried to speak normal.

Isabelle turned her head to see the clock. Constantin licked his lips without realizing it and then instantly regretted it. He didn't want her to think he was a slobbery kisser.

"Five," she murmured.

Constantin thought he might faint. This wasn't his first kiss, but he sure was acting like he'd never kissed a girl before. Maybe he was freaking out because she was famous. "Four," he whispered back.

"Three." Isabelle didn't turn her head back to him yet, but she leaned a little closer.

"Two."

"One."

Isabelle turned and kissed him.

Isabelle realized her mistake the moment their lips touched. This wasn't just a kiss to distract a boy until she incapacitated him, this was a Kiss. With a capital K. This wasn't Constantin's first kiss, either, although she had been a bit worried that it might be. Once he'd gotten over his initial timidity, the kiss deepened until tongues got involved, until one kiss had turned into an unending series of kisses.

When Isabelle's brain started working again, she had her arms wrapped around Constantin's neck and his arms held her against him. The Kiss had gone on too long and hadn't been long enough. She broke their lips apart and gasped for air as if she'd been running a marathon.

"Oh, wow," said Constantin, clearly feeling as thrown as she did.

Isabelle shook her head, unable to speak. She loosened her grip on his neck despite wanting to pull him closer and kiss him again.

"Are you okay?" Constantin started to ask. He opened his mouth to say more, but she didn't let him. She barely had enough resolve to go through with her mission as it was. She couldn't let him show her again what a great guy he was. She ran her right hand over his shoulder and before he could react pinched his Carotid artery.

Constantin sagged to the ground, instantly unconscious.

Isabelle made sure he wasn't laying on something uncomfortable before heading to the desk to see if she could find the gun-runner's laptop. She didn't rush. Although she'd never had to use the Pond Pinch in the field before, she had used it a number of times at parties when some of her "friends" got too drunk to remember the meaning of the word "no." Based on previous experience, she knew she had at least a half hour before Constantin would begin to stir.

Pulling on a pair of latex gloves she had hidden in her bra, she rummaged through the room's desk until she found Constantin's father's laptop. The gun-runner was paranoid, with reason, and this particular computer had no internet capabilities. Since it also held all his contacts, his inventory, and his sales, copying the data on it was a high BND priority. She rammed a special USB flash drive into one of the computer's ports. The BND techs had preloaded the drive with an automatic program that began downloading the contents of the computer immediately.

She watched the screen for a moment while the data started copying to the drive. Schematics of various weapons, some even she didn't recognize, flashed up and then away as the data transferred. Isabelle smiled, pleased at her mission's success.

"What are you doing?" Constantin asked.

Constantin wasn't sure what was going on. One minute he was enjoying the best kiss of his life, and the next he was on the floor with a sore shoulder. Isabelle stood over his father's sacred never-to-be-touched computer. Her face paled for a moment, and then her mouth set in a hard line. Her eyes narrowed.

"Of course," she said. "You're not drunk. The pinch must be more effective if you're drunk."

"What?" Constantin climbed to his feet, a little unsteady both from the kiss and passing out and from the gibberish coming from Isabelle's mouth. "What are you doing with Dad's computer? I mean, I know he's

A Princess, a Mission, and a Kiss 63

got his business stuff on there but why would a princess care about the amount of wheat Dad imported into Hungary last year?"

Isabelle's jaw dropped open. "You don't know?" Her eyes scanned his face like she was looking for something. Constantin felt more confused by the minute.

"You really don't know." Isabelle sort of sagged against the desk. "You really think your dad is some kind of …" She paused as if the words she wanted floated just out of reach. "Some kind of grocer."

"He's more than that," Constantin said, not sure why he was bothering to defend his father. Still, it was one thing for him to think poorly of the head of the Corvins. It was quite another thing for this upstart royal (even if she was the most fantastic kisser) to denigrate Constantin's father.

"I'll say." Isabelle flipped the computer around so he could see the screen. Bizarre photos blinked on and off the screen almost faster than he could process. He did recognize the nuclear hazard symbol on one of the images as it flashed by.

"Was?" Constantin tried to swallow, but his throat seemed to have stopped working. "Was that a nuke?"

Isabelle shrugged as if she saw this kind of thing

every day. "Probably."

Now Constantin was the one sagging against the desk. "Why is this on my dad's computer?" he whispered.

Isabelle bit her lip for a second. It brought back the memory of their kiss, but Constantin shook his head and pushed the memory away. "I don't know how to tell you this," she said, "but your dad is one of the largest, most influential arms dealers in the world."

Constantin just stared. He wanted to argue, to protest, to tell Isabelle she couldn't possibly know, but the evidence flashed across his father's screen. The proof was in his father's weird business associates, people Constantin had always thought to be a strange fit for the food importing business. Did a glorified grocer like his father really need twenty bodyguards surrounding his home at all times?

"Who are you?" he asked her instead of continuing with those disturbing thoughts.

Isabelle gave him a sort of half-hearted laugh filled with cynicism instead of humor. "I'm a princess of Neubaden who takes the duty of protecting my people a little further than most."

"Your people?" He raised his eyebrows at her.

This time her laugh sounded a bit more genuine.

"My people. It's true that they might not have much use for princes and princesses in this day and age, but that doesn't mean my duty and loyalty should cease." She pulled a tiny flash drive out of the computer and pushed the laptop shut. Pulling off the latex gloves he hadn't noticed on her hands, she stuffed them and the drive down the front of her dress. There was no way he was going to try to get that drive back now.

"I would lay down my life for them," Isabelle continued, "which I may have just done. If you tell your father about what I just did, he will have me killed."

Constantin opened his mouth to protest, but then snapped it shut without saying a word. Two years ago, his dad had caught him making out with the second foreign minister's daughter. The minister had rapidly lost his post, and his whole family, including the daughter, had moved to London. His dad had insisted it was for the best since "that girl" hadn't been good enough for a Corvin. Only, that girl had disappeared from social media, and not even her best friend had heard from her after the move. Constantin had always kind of wondered.

God, he'd been so blind.

"I'm sorry you had to learn the truth this way." Isabelle reached over to pat his arm, but he snatched it away.

"So, all this." He pointed at the two of them. "All of it was just an act to get access to my father's computer."

"That kiss was not an act." She touched her lips for a moment as if she too had been moved by that kiss, as if she'd also found it to be as momentous as he had.

Constantin didn't say anything. There was nothing left to be said.

Isabelle moved to the door. She had her hand on the knob, ready to twist it open when she turned back. Giving him one of her brightest smiles, she said, "If your father doesn't have me killed, I'll see you in school in three weeks." Then she winked. She. Winked.

Still reeling from the audacity, Constantin didn't notice when Isabelle left the room. The click of the door shutting brought him back to the present.

With a sigh, he walked around the desk and put the computer back in the drawer where his dad had stashed it before the ball, erasing the last bit of evidence that Isabelle had messed with it. He stared around the room. The furniture hadn't changed, yet his world had. His father was a gun runner; the best kiss of his life was some sort of spy.

He sank down on the uncomfortable chair behind the desk and sighed. Three weeks, she had said. He began to smile. He couldn't wait.

Lori Bond is the code name for an author of teen books featuring spies, crooks, and those who want to be spies or crooks. She lives somewhere on this Earth (as opposed to another world in the multiverse) with people she claims are her family. For more books, her newsletter, and information, visit her at covertreads.com.

Princess Deneige

Susan Bianculli

I never expected to be running for my life at only fifteen. I am Princess Deneige—"the snow" in French, if you're wondering—and though my upbringing wasn't conventional for royalty, still I never even dreamed that I would become a princess in peril. Actually, make that a princess in mortal danger. I survived two attempts on my life in as many days, and I knew who was behind it, too.

Royalty or not, my life hadn't been pampered and spoiled. My parents, King Eriik and Queen Arcadia, had told me since I was old enough to understand words that I needed to be a "proper" Princess; that I needed to learn about Life as well as academics so that in the future I could be a good future ruler for my people. But what was "proper" changed with every nanny hired. One thought "proper" was sitting quietly and doing needlework. Her successor thought that "proper" meant learning how to clean my bedroom and make it shine. A long list of nannies came and went over the years, in addition to my tutors, to fulfil my parents' plans for my education.

I was eleven when that changed. My mother died suddenly after coming down with a sickness, and while we were still in shock, a royal cousin on my father's side of the family, Elspeth, came to the castle to take care of my father and me. It was nice to have someone to handle social duties for us while we were grieving my mother's loss, but it wasn't long afterwards that I'd been told by my father that Elspeth was to become my new stepmother. He'd tried to explain that I needed a mother and the kingdom needed a queen, but I think he just needed to have someone living beside him that wasn't a daughter.

In short order my older, wrinkled, grey-haired and grey-eyed father and younger, beautiful, blonde-haired and blue-eyed Elspeth were married in a grand royal ceremony. But if I'd thought my life had been difficult before, it became unbearable almost immediately after the wedding reception ended. My stepmother started putting me to work. Real work. My academic tutors and my last nanny were dismissed, and instead I was given a stern "instructor" named Old Johann. His only duty was to oversee me in all kinds of household chores and to "instruct" me in a task when I did something wrong. Those frequently had involved lots of tiresome repetition of a task when I made a mistake, no matter how small; nor did it matter if I quickly corrected it. I had to start again, and do all the repetitions decreed by him. The palace servants, pitying me, had tried to help whenever they could, but they were often blocked in their attempts by Johann.

I'd tried complaining to my father multiple times, but he would only vacantly pat my head and say things like "But if you already know how to do that, what's the problem?" and "Come come, now, you're exaggerating," and stuff like that. He didn't understand, or maybe didn't want to understand, that I had become little more than a servant and wasn't learning anything that I would need to be a future queen.

One positive outcome, though, was that I'd became very fit and slender since I was kept on the run morning, noon, and night. Of course, since I too ate the kinds of foods my father and step-mother ate when I had my meals with them at my father's request, I also remained healthy. Another positive outcome was that I'd figured out how to balance my work against each other to help myself. For example, the harsh soaps I used in my cleaning were balanced out by the butters and oils I put on my skin from baking and cooking. But I couldn't understand why my new stepmother, instead of continuing to look at me smugly as I did my chores around her, seemed more and more sour as the years passed.

I found out why the hard way.

Four years later, I'd just had my fifteenth birthday and was sweeping in the throne room when I heard voices coming from the little study that was behind a hidden door in back of the throne. At that time of day no one should have been in there, and we had no visitors in the palace, royal or otherwise. So of course I was curious. I pressed my ear to the thin wooden door to listen. I distinctly heard my stepmother speaking angrily to someone. I almost wish now that I didn't hear it, but my life would have been very much the shorter if I hadn't.

"How is it that Deneige continues to thrive?" she'd spat venomously. "I've given her all the hardest tasks, and still she looks much the same as she did four years ago, except somehow more beautiful. Ugh! I should be the fairest of them all, not her!"

A male voice rumbled a reply which I couldn't hear,

and she'd said in turn, "No, I can't put her in with the servants, much as I would like that. Her father would miss her, and the servants would only protect her more than they try to now. Since the King is besotted with me, he doesn't listen to her complaints, and thinks things are like they have always been in terms of her 'life lessons.' But if Deneige weren't around, her father would look for her. And then maybe actually listen to her."

Another male rumble, and she said, suddenly sounding pleased, "Yeeesss. It needs to look like an accident. It has been long enough since her mother's death. But it can't be connected to me."

I grew dizzy and leaned against the door. I had always assumed that Elspeth really didn't like me, from the snide comments about my appearance to her refusal to touch me after she had been crowned Queen. But to hear her actively plot my death was shocking. Footsteps approached the door, and I'd hurried to duck out of sight behind the throne. Peeping up over the gold scrolled arm rest, I saw my stepmother in a set of gorgeous royal purple robes sweep haughtily from the study. She'd been followed by her brown leather-clad huntsman, a harsh man hired by her directly. I gulped quietly, because he was trouble.

He was her eyes and ears when in the palace, and had license to go everywhere except the royal bedrooms. If I was to not die, I knew I would need to be on the lookout from now on.

Not long afterwards the first of the attempts on my life happened. I'd been scrubbing the cooking utensils in the huge tin tub in the wash room when hard hands shoved me in the middle of my back. I screamed as I went flying into the tub, soapy bubbles filling my mouth, and a sharp knife propped upright but hidden under the soap suds sliced my shoulder as I fell on it. I was quickly pulled up by Wash Mistress Marion; and when it was discovered I was bleeding, she'd bandaged me up.

"There now, Princess. Are you all right?" Marion had asked me with a worried tone, securing the bandage in place. "Perhaps you could sneak up to your room and have a lie-down. Don't worry, we'll cover for you with Johann."

"How could this have happened?" I asked, shaken at my narrow escape. A couple of inches more to the right and it would have gone into my neck, not across the top of my shoulder.

She'd frowned. "I don't rightly know. It does seem strange, but I guess accidents can happen anywhere."

Coincidence that this occurred the day after the huntsman talked to my stepmother? Probably not. My stepmother had said it needed to look like an accident. And she had been speaking to her huntsman. And I remembered that I'd seen him leaving the washroom as I was carrying plates inside. It had to have been him who'd set up the knife, and who must have snuck back in to push me.

The second attempt came the day after that. I'd been in the kitchen baking the strawberry tarts my father loved so much, and saw a shadow block the sun from the little window up high in the stone walls behind me. Instinct kicked in, and I'd whirled away from the fireplace as if I had just remembered to get a particular spice when the huntsman "accidentally" stumbled right where I had been. Had I not moved, I definitely would have fallen—or been pushed—into the fire. Instead, he nearly fell into the flames. The cook nearest me rushed to help him stay upright.

"Are you all right?" I'd asked the huntsman, turning to face him with as much wide eyed innocence as I could manage.

He looked at me levelly before replying, "I am fine," and leaving. That tore it. I knew then he really *was* going to try and kill me no matter who was around!

After finishing with the tarts and reporting in to Johann, who no longer physically followed me around, I'd gone to my room. I'd paced its thick flowered carpet and tried to decide what I was less afraid of: leaving the castle to save my life but having nowhere to go and no way to take care of myself, or staying and trying to avoid being killed while having a roof over my head, food to eat, and clothes to wear. I knew I couldn't go to my father, because my stepmother had been right. He wouldn't listen to me, probably thinking it all some sort of teenaged temper tantrum. But near-deadly accidents twice in two days had left me rattled and scared that a third attempt would be successful.

I decided to leave the castle right away. I packed a small basket, the kind I would use when sent out to gather flowers for the family rooms, and hid a few things in it like soap, a comb, some of the tarts I'd baked, and some gold coins under the light cloak I always took with me. I then dressed in my sturdiest grey work dress, white apron, and black knee boots. I couldn't avoid castle servants or guards on my way out, but they paid me no notice once they saw the flower basket. I breathed easier when I stepped off the draw bridge, but was also struck with a sudden sadness. I already missed my father and all the people with whom I'd grown up. I didn't miss the recent additions to the castle, though.

I forced myself into a carefree skip as I headed out to the fields where I often picked flowers because I didn't want to draw suspicion with any changes in my behavior. As soon as I was out of sight I ran straight for the forest on the far side of the meadows. It was the perfect place for me to hide while I figured out what to do with myself even though I'd always been warned to not go there because it was dangerous.

It may be dangerous there, but being back in the castle was more perilous, I reasoned.

I hadn't been five minutes in the woods when something prompted me to look back over my shoulder at the meadow. My heart stopped a moment, and then it started galloping wildly.

The huntsman was running towards the forest.

I whirled and sprinted further in, throwing my basket to the ground behind me so it wouldn't weigh me down. He crashed in among the trees, sacrificing stealth for speed. Since he was full grown with longer legs, he was catching up fast. But I had speed borne of terror, and being smaller I could slip through the tangled places much easier than he could. Thankfully I managed to lose him. Knowing that he would stop and track me I was very glad to soon stumble across a small brook. I jumped in and waded upstream so that he would lose my trail, and stayed walking in the water until I lost feeling in my submerged body parts. I got out by climbing a grey-brown tree whose roots were halfway in the water and went as high in the branches as I dared. I took off my boots and rubbed feeling back into my legs and feet, slumping tiredly against the broad trunk. I closed my eyes for what I thought was just a second, and the next thing I knew it was night.

I woke up hungry and thirsty. Thirsty I fixed by cupping water into my hands from the stream, but eating was another story. A faint aroma of meat being cooked came from somewhere and I was hungry enough to want to find its source. I put my boots back on and followed my nose to a hidden little glen with a small house with a kitchen garden and a little pond. The delicious smell came from the chimney's smoke. Taking my courage in both hands I walked up to the door and knocked.

A gruff voice from inside called out, "Who's there?"

"A lost traveler who has lost her belongings and is in need of charity." I crossed my fingers and prayed that the gruff voice was paired with a kind soul.

Abruptly the door was flung open. The people inside and I gaped at each other. I saw seven little men about three feet high with long beards of differing colors standing in the doorway, and beyond them was a rather chaotic, messy-looking house.

"You're young to be a-travelling alone, missy," the one in front, who was probably the leader, finally said.

"But pretty as a princess!" sighed a voice in the back. "With hair as black as night, lips as red as blood, and skin as white as snow."

I froze. Those were the words my mother had used in the explanation of my name to me when I was little. *Did they somehow know who I was? And if so, how?*

"Quiet, Arrik," scoffed another. "No princesses would be wandering around the woods at night dressed like that and without bodyguards. Idjit."

"Please?" I begged, mentally breathing a sigh of relief that they didn't really know who I was. "I would be willing to do work in exchange for a meal and a place to stay for tonight."

"Where are your parents?" asked the leader.

"My mother's dead," I said, which was the truth.

"Aww, let her in, Garrin. She can't possibly harm us," said another voice.

"Yeah!" the others chorused.

Garrin sighed. "All right. You can come in. What's your name?"

"Umm, Snow—Snow, uh, White," I invented.

"All right, Snow. Can you cook?"

"I can."

"Good. You can finish up the dinner we've started. Help yourself to any ingredients you find in the pantry in the kitchen."

From what I could find, I decided to make a spicy meat and vegetable stew from the meat turning by itself on the magical spit in the fireplace, and serve it up with toasted day-old bread with the help of one knife that cut the bread by itself and another that spread butter on contact.

How much easier my castle chores would have been if I'd had some of these magical tools, I thought enviously.

The seven little men—introduced to me as Arrik, Kort, Frantz, Berg, Jarman, Garrin, and Hanz—enjoyed my meal so much that after dinner an arrangement was struck between us: I could stay as long as I wanted in exchange for cooking and cleaning. I immediately accepted.

The next morning, after the little men had left to work in the mine they owned, I got to work. I had just begun on the amazing pile of dirty dishes in the sink when a pounding sounded on the front door. Afraid, I immediately dropped to the floor and crawled under the kitchen worktable.

"Open up in the name of the Queen!" came a harsh voice from outside.

My heart raced. The huntsman!

How did he find me? I wondered.

He pounded some more but finally stopped. I stayed hidden. A shadow crossed the floor of the kitchen, and I realized he was peering in the windows. I held very still, hardly daring to breathe. The shadow disappeared but I didn't move for a good hour or more. I only came out when my muscles protested their cramped position. I snuck over to each of the windows of the house and peeked out, breathing a sigh of relief when I didn't see anyone anywhere outside. I went back to work and managed to make a decent dent in the household chores before the little men came home to the dinner I had ready on the table.

Halfway through the meal, Garrin asked me between bites, "Anything unusual happen today?"

"Ummmm…"

He raised a red eyebrow kindly at me, and for some reason that was enough for the floodgates to open. They all listened, astonished, as I put down my fork and knife and poured out my story from the time my mother died right up to the time I knocked on their door, and then broke down sobbing. They gathered around trying to soothe me, and eventually I was able to stop crying.

"Don't worry, Princess Deneige. Our bargain will still hold. And what's more, we will make sure that you'll be protected from your stepmother," Garrin assured me as the others chimed in, agreeing.

At that moment a pounding started up on the door again. I put my hands to my mouth, eyes wide, as I heard the huntsman's voice order angrily, "Open in the name of the Queen!"

"Quick, under the table," whispered Hanz to me, and I scurried under it as most of the little men seated themselves again to help hide me. Only Garrin went to answer the door.

"Have you seen a young runaway serving girl?" the

huntsman demanded as soon as the door was open.

Garrin just looked at him. "Why should I tell you?"

"I am the Queen's personal servitor, and I order you to tell me if you have seen a young, black-haired runaway servant!"

The leader of the little men frowned. "How do I know that you are who you say you are? Have you any proof?"

The huntsman towered over Garrin threateningly. "I am bigger and stronger than you are, little man, so tell me what I want to know or you'll feel my wrath."

I was instantly afraid. I didn't want Garrin or any of the others getting hurt on my account, but I also knew what would happen if I revealed myself. I saw the huntsman raise a fist aggressively in the air. That decided me.

"Stop!" I shrieked. "Don't kill him!" I scrambled out from under the table between Frantz and Berg's chairs. Though I knew it would mean my death, I also knew I wouldn't be able to live with myself if any of the little men sacrificed their lives for mine.

"Ah-ha! There you are!" he said triumphantly. He glanced at Garrin. "And for harboring a wanted runaway, you little men will be taken into custody!"

"You mean 'harboring a princess', don't you?" Garrin said dryly.

The huntsman scowled, realizing I had told them everything and had been believed. He pushed forward to grab me, but Garrin stuck his foot out and the huntsman went crashing to the wooden floor. Immediately all the little men leapt up from their seats and dog-piled on him, pinning him down.

"Get off me," he bellowed, struggling against their weight.

"Princess! In the washroom down the hall there is a white cabinet. Get the purple ceramic jar out and bring it back here! Hurry!" Garrin commanded.

I ran to bring back the requested jar, and Garrin rubbed some of the orange goop inside it on the back of the huntsman's neck. His struggles immediately started getting weaker, and within a couple of minutes he was snoring on the floor. The little men got off him, and Garrin bent down to whisper something in his ear. Then he stood to answer the silent questions written on my face.

"This is a jar of magic ointment that was given to us in barter for some of our ore. That's how we've gotten all of the magical tools we have. He will wake with the memory of what I whispered: that he found you and killed you. That will spare you from being hunted again." Garrin smiled.

I couldn't help but smile back as Jarmann, Kort, Frantz, and Hanz picked up the sleeping huntsman and took him to dump him far away in the woods.

A year passed, and I lived very happily with the seven little men. All the training that my parents had given me really paid off during this time. I cooked, and cleaned, and sewed while they worked their mine and brought in supplies. One crisp fall day, not long after my sixteenth birthday, I was out in the woods about a mile from the house gathering berries to make a berry pie. A crunching of underbrush startled me, and an old woman came out from behind a bush with a basket of apples over her arm.

"Oh, dearie! I am a poor apple peddler that has lost her way in the woods. Can you show me how to get to the road again?"

There was no road for several miles from the bushes' location. She would have had to force her way through some pretty rough terrain to get to where we were. This made me suspicious.

"Actually, I'm not sure," I lied. "And I don't want to get lost myself, so I will have to wish you luck on your own. I'm sorry."

The old woman frowned, then tried again. "Oh, but dearie, I am such an old bag of bones. It would be sweet of you to help me. I'll even give you an apple from my basket as payment?"

She reached in and then held out the most delicious looking apple I'd ever seen. Apples were my favorite, and apple trees didn't grow in those woods. Plus it had been some time since the little men had brought any apples home from the closest village's market day. My mouth watered.

"Go on, take it!" she urged, but something about her face made me think about Elspeth for the first time in months. I looked closer at the old woman. It was my stepmother in disguise!

"No!" I screamed, and dropped my burlap berry bag as I fled into the woods.

"You won't escape me, Deneige! I too have magic now! That's how I knew you'd enchanted my huntsman and that you were still alive! But I'll change that!" she yelled angrily, throwing away her basket to chase me.

I ran as hard as I could towards the center of the

forest where the foothills leading to the mine was located, knowing the little men would help me. I dashed up the steep path beside the deep-pooled waterfall with her right behind me and screaming that she was going to make me die.

Then the fact that she hadn't even shown me a weapon before I started running caught up with my brain. I screeched to a halt and whirled around to face her, suddenly angry at myself; angry at her; angry at the whole situation.

"What in the world is the matter with you!?" I yelled.

Elspeth stopped short three feet away, confusion replacing the maniacal anger on her face for a moment.

"Why are you even here? You've driven me from the castle, and from my father, to live deep in the forest away from people. Nobody outside of this forest even knows I'm still alive! Can't you be content with that? Why do you even care? Why do you have to kill me now?" I shouted at her.

"Because as long as you are alive, you are the fairest of them all! And that's not fair!" she yelled back, stamping her foot in a temper tantrum.

My mouth dropped open. "What?" I finally managed to gasp.

"I want to be the fairest of them all! I want everyone to look at me, and be awed at my beauty, and do anything I ask of them just because I am beautiful!"

"You know that you are considered lovely by everyone. And you've been the Queen for four years. You have both beauty *and* power," I said, no longer shouting. "People already do anything you ask because of both of those things. And even if I was more beautiful, what does it matter? There are no villagers, castle servants, guardsmen, or anyone like that out here to see me and compare me to you. Why would they even *do* that, anyway?"

Elspeth opened her mouth, and then closed it. I pressed on.

"Is beauty really the be-all and end-all for you? Looks fade, you know. My father, when he was young, was a very handsome man. Or so the portrait of him in the Great Hall shows. He is still good-looking, but he doesn't look the way he used to anymore. What people care about from him, and will remember him for, is that he has been a just and fair ruler. Wouldn't it be better for you to become known for something like kindness, or being a really good falcon hunter, or a great embroiderer, or something else that lasts beyond looks?" I asked.

She cocked her head to the side, then said in a cold voice, "You do have a point. Yes, you live out here where no one sees you. But someone may come into the forest, or you might leave it. Even if you swore to me that wouldn't happen, still I will know that you live and are more beautiful than me."

I was stunned that she completely dismissed all the rest of my arguments. Was she really that single-minded? Elspeth advanced towards me, fingers shaping themselves into claws as if she was already anticipating them wrapped around my neck. I saw, however, that there was still no weapon in either hand.

"Do you really expect me to let you kill me without a fight?" I asked, falling into a copy of a defensive position I'd seen guardsmen do in the castle practice yard.

"Yes!"

She rushed at me, and we grappled there on the path beside the waterfall. She maneuvered me closer and closer to the edge, and I understood that she was going to try and push me over it. I tried to stop it from happening, but her magic made her stronger than me. The nearer we got to the edge, the more the ground grew slick under our boots. I was frantic. I didn't want to die! Elspeth's boots suddenly shot out from under her and she slipped halfway over the cliff, her legs dangling above the waterfall's gorge. I dug my feet into the ground and leaned back, not wanting her to take me with her if she fell. Elspeth growled and gripped frantically at my sleeves, but the shoulder lacings that fastened my sleeves to my blouse ripped through the fabric and she fell out of sight with a scream. I collapsed to my knees to catch my breath before I was brave enough to look over the edge. I discovered she'd fallen only about fifteen feet, still holding my sleeves, down onto a rock outcropping below. But she wasn't moving. Just then the little men came running down the path.

"Princess!" "What are you doing here?" "Are you all right?" "Jarmann told us he heard screaming while on guard duty!" they shouted in worried tones as they crowded around me.

I told them what had happened, and then I started crying. All the stress of running for my life, and loathing of my stepmother, and fear of being killed caught up with me. Half of them stayed to comfort me and let me cry myself out, and the other half climbed down to check on Elspeth.

"She'll be fine," Garrin called up to me after looking

her over. "She's just knocked out cold."

It was kind of weird, but I was relieved she wasn't dead. She may have wanted to kill me, but she was my father's wife after all. And I didn't want him to be lonely. But I also didn't want to have her continuing to try and kill me once she woke up. A brilliant idea popped into my head at that, which stopped my crying.

"Hey, Garrin? I know she's unconscious right now, but is there a way to keep her unconscious for a little while longer?" I called down to him.

Garrin looked at me with raised eyebrows but unquestioningly took out a dagger from his leg sheath and carefully hit Elspeth on the lower back part of the skull with its pommel.

I jumped to my feet. "Wait here. I'll be back in about half an hour!" I said gaily to the little men, who all stared at me in astonishment.

I raced to the cottage, got from the medicine cabinet the jar of magical orange goop that had been used on the huntsman, and raced back again.

"Here! Catch!" I said, tossing the ceramic container down to Garrin.

The little men all smiled, now understanding. Garrin opened the jar, swiped the ointment across the back of Elspeth's neck and said something in her ear before pocketing the container again. I knew that he'd whispered pretty much the same thing that he'd told the huntsman: that she'd caught me and killed me. That, plus the ripped sleeves from my blouse left behind as a kind of proof, would put an end to her looking for me.

"That's that, Snow," Garrin said, as he and the rest of the little men gathered around me. "Let's go home, where you are welcome to stay forever if you wish."

I sighed with relief. I knew I could never go back to the castle and my father now, but at least I would always have a secure home

Susan Bianculli wears the titles "Mother" and "Wife" most proudly. Another is "Author" for *The Mist Gate Crossings* series, as well as several short stories in several other anthologies.

Check out susanbianculli.wix.com/home for more information.

Becoming

Kath Boyd Marsh

Olivia's youngest cousin Kat paced her chamber as the other princesses arrived. Kat held a scroll in her hand. Olivia, her sister Lisette, and Kat's sister Melinda looked at each other. Seeing Kat excited about something she'd *read* was new. In fact Olivia couldn't remember another time when she'd seen Kat read.

"What ...?" Melinda started to ask her younger sister.

Kat waved the scroll at the other three. "I found it. Our next adventure! *And* a way to help the farmers."

"What farmers?" Lisette asked.

"All the farmers! Their crops are failing. Don't you pay attention?" Kat's face was scarlet, almost matching her dark red curls. Her quick temper helped with her swordplay and gave her power her five feet of height belied, but passion could make her unintelligible too.

Melinda captured Kat's flailing arm and said gently, "Kat, slowly, tell us about the farmers."

Kat looked to Olivia.

"Yesterday we may have overheard Father and the Council talking about crops failing." Olivia plucked her dagger out of its sheath and ran a finger along the edge of her blade as if testing to see if it might need sharpening.

"By overheard, you mean you and Kat spied on the Council Chamber from that hidden passage you found?" Lisette tugged the dagger out of Olivia's hand and stared at her younger sister.

"Gathering information," Olivia said holding out her hand for her dagger. She did not know where Kat had gone after they'd left the secret passage. Apparently from the scroll she was waving about, her unpredictable cousin had headed to the castle library.

Kat shook the scroll again. "Come on, people. This is our chance to not just sit around talking about how great we were defeating trolls two months ago. We have a new chance to do something at least as great." She held up the parchment again. "*AND* it involves dragons!"

A shiver raced down Olivia's back. She remembered the word *becoming* echoing in her head and the feeling in her body when they had battled the trolls. Her arms had felt like they were becoming wings at the same time they were still her arms … and her breath … she could swear she'd breathed fire. But no one had said a thing about her or about seeing a dragon. All the talk around the castle had been about four mysterious knights who had defeated the Trolls at the tournament.

"Dragons and crops?" Melinda asked. She was the best archer of the four princesses, who after their success at being more than just pretty musicians and artists, now called themselves The Perilous Princesses.

It had started six months ago, when the four cousins were working on embroidery and complaining about how bored they were and how interesting their bro-thers' lives were. Since they were little, their brothers had trained to be knights who could go out and kill monsters while the princesses were only supposed to faint. For years the princesses had secretly practiced what they had seen their brothers learn.

Now they needed more. Olivia had come up with a plan and had gone to her father and pled with him for dagger throwing lessons. King George had sighed. "Of course you aren't like your sister or your cousins. You won't leave me be until I say yes. So, yes."

It wasn't the first time he'd complained that she would never be a kind of perfect lady princess like her sister, and Olivia had counted on it. That day King

George arranged for the Weapons Master to instruct Olivia.

At that first lesson, she convinced the Weapons Master to train all four princesses to handle many kinds of weapons. Olivia was best with a dagger: throwing, stabbing. Kat was a scary good swords-woman. Gentle tall Melinda pulled back her golden curls and shot a bow and arrow like she was born to it. Lisette, Olivia's frills and lace older sister, turned out to be pretty good at everything, but mostly so fast on her feet Olivia bet Lisette could beat their oldest brother Ian in a race.

After training for four months, the princesses decided to participate in the annual All-Kingdoms Tournament. They'd each designed armor. Kat wore a plain silver she felt was sleek and right for a swords-woman. Melinda and Lisette both chose gold, not a surprise for such feminine princesses. Olivia couldn't say why, but she had to have a burnished black. When she first put it on, it felt like a second skin instead of bulky heavy metal.

On the day of the tournament, Lisette had fussed over a missing feather for her helmet, making them late for the tournament games. Olivia had finally plucked her own feather out and handed it to her sister. But their lateness meant the contests were almost over, and most of the knights were resting either from exhaustion or wounds.

And then the Trolls attacked. The princesses were the ones who stood and fought.

Once the Trolls were defeated, the princesses escaped before anyone could discover their real identities. Four teenaged princesses were supposed to be in the stands waving tokens for the knights they supported, not cutting down Trolls. Even if the king had been pleased, their mothers would have found a way to prevent them from ever being in that kind of danger again.

They were so happy with themselves that the next day they formed The Perilous Princesses. Every day when they were supposed to be painting pictures or doing embroidery, they met and took weapons lessons. Until today nothing had happened that excited the foursome. There'd been no reason to get out their armor once again and fight.

For the first time since the tournament, Olivia felt her skin crawl, and again that word whispered in her ear: *Becoming*. Over the past two months she'd been in the castle library reading everything she could find about dragons. She hadn't come across the particular scroll

Kat was holding. "Could I see the scroll?" she asked.

Kat handed it over. Olivia read it. She was almost half way through when impatient Kat jabbed the parchment. "There. Look. It says dragons left behind a treasure, and there's a dragon power stone. Everybody knows dragons could do more magic than wizards. They could make rain out of a drop of water using one of their power stones. We can use one to get rain or whatever the farmers need." She threw back her shoulders. "Only The Perilous Princesses can defeat a dragon and bring the magic stone back!" She grinned. "Well, find the stone, since dragons are dead."

Melinda and Lisette crowded in. "How can we do it?" Being seventeen, they weren't as rash as fifteen-year-old Olivia and Kat.

The cold on Olivia's neck got colder. It wasn't fear, but something was wrong. She felt it in the skin of the scroll itself. She rolled it back up and looked at the seal Kat had broken to read it. "Where did you get this?" She had a bad idea.

"In that room with all the good stuff they don't want princesses to read," Kat said as if it was obvious. "We'll use it to save the farmers!"

"The locked room?" Olivia knew which room Kat meant, but she wanted her suspicion to be wrong.

Kat looked up, down, shrugged. "Yes. You have a problem with that?"

What was done was done. Olivia shook her head and unrolled the scroll again and read to the end while the other three princesses chirped their excitement. "Did you read the entire thing?" she finally asked.

Kat shrugged. "I read enough."

"Not quite. There's a curse here. I don't know about getting a magic stone, but we will definitely be battling at least one dragon. The only question is how fast do we tell Father." Olivia scanned her sister's and cousins' faces. But not one of them nodded.

Lisette finally asked. "Okay. Tell us why."

Olivia pointed to the last line on the scroll. "It says, 'By the reading of this scroll, the dragon is released.'"

For a moment there was dead silence. Then Kat laughed. "No way. Dragons are extinct. Everybody knows that. The scroll has a map to their treasure. All we have to do is go get it."

Olivia was surprised when Melinda and Lisette shrugged and nodded agreement with Kat. But then Lisette held up her left hand and wiggled her fingers.

Melinda grabbed her hand, exclaiming, "Lisette! When did you get engaged?" Melinda's betrothal had been announced the month before. Her eyes shown with happiness as she held Lisette's hand. The two older cousins were so much alike. They'd both fallen in love.

Kat and Olivia groaned. At fifteen, Olivia thought boys were mostly irritating. And neither she nor Kat really liked dress balls. There definitely would be plenty now to celebrate.

Lisette blushed. "Willum proposed last night. The announcement will be at the ball tonight."

Olivia and Kat groaned again. There was no way they could dodge this party now.

The whole dragon thing was forgotten as the princesses prepared for the evening's ball—forgotten by all except Olivia. She couldn't shake off the feeling that something dark and huge lurked over them. The others might not believe there were dragons, but she couldn't shake the deep feeling that the scroll might really release a dragon. And it didn't make her feel any better to remember feeling like one. She needed to talk to her father, but when she tried, he brushed her off. Everybody was too busy with the ball that had turned into an engagement celebration.

Olivia was bored all through the party. Her appetite, usually good, was gone because she could not forget the dragon curse. What would happen? Would the curse turn someone into a dragon? Her? Was she crazy to think she had felt like a dragon at the tournament? Finally the worry was too much. She slipped out of the hall into the formal gardens. Sitting by her favorite fountain, she let the falling water soothe her.

When at last she felt relaxed, her eyes heavy, someone sat down beside her. She jerked upright and saw her distant cousin Henry. If she hadn't recognized the way he brushed his hair out of his eyes, she would never have recognized him. Until he'd arrived for the ball, he had not been to the castle since he was a drippy-nosed youngster who deliberately wiped his face on the back of her best tunic. He'd been a pest who trailed behind her like a lost wolfhound.

That had been years ago. Olivia was glad to see those years had not been wasted. His nose no longer dripped. His hair was sleek and golden, except for his unruly bangs, pulled back and tied with a leather strap almost as brown as his eyes. He laughed at her stare, and that laugh rang like deep chapel bells.

She thought about watching him in the Hall, before she realized it was Henry. Every unmarried girl at the party had gathered around him. He'd never once looked at Olivia.

Now he leaned back, dangerously close to falling into the fountain. "You are missing a very good party. My brother Willum and your sister look seriously happy."

Olivia shrugged. "Duh. They're going to get married." She spit the words out before she could bite back her bitterness. She dreaded the day Lisette and Melinda got married and The Perilous Princesses dissolved. Even Kat had an admirer, Michael. Luckily at only fifteen like Olivia, marriage was years away.

Henry laughed again, and her stomach felt weirdly jumpy and her throat oddly dry. "I take it you don't approve of marriage?"

"I didn't say that. I just think no one needs to rush into getting married."

But Henry seemed bored already. He stared at Gracella, the princess from Gardenshire, who bore down on them like a hound on the hunt.

"There you are, Henry. The last dance is about to begin. You promised."

He stood bowing to Gracella. Before he walked

away, Henry winked at Olivia and said, "Becoming."

Olivia jumped to her feet. That word again. "What do you mean becoming?" she demanded.

Gracella giggled. "He was talking about my gown, weren't you, Henry?"

He smiled at Gracella, then turned back for a second and winked at Olivia again.

She didn't know what he meant, and she didn't care. She was pretty sure.

The next day, only Olivia got up early for lessons with the Weaponry Master. He looked like he wished he'd stayed in bed like everyone else, but Olivia was intent. Her sister and Melinda mediated when they were bothered, but for Olivia relaxing meant dagger throwing. She managed to hit her target dead center ten times out of ten. Her shoulders began to unknot until—

"Seems you need a more difficult target."

Olivia turned to order the Weaponry Master to get a smaller one or put this hay-stuffed target farther away, but the Master had dozed off leaning against a column.

Henry stood behind her grinning. "Good morn, cousin," he said in that voice that made Olivia feel like something was happening that she was not prepared for. A new feeling, or at least one she hadn't had before yesterday.

"Can you throw better?" she snapped.

He shrugged. "Perhaps." He walked to the target and pulled out her dagger, balancing it in his palm. "Nice." He stopped beside her, turned, and without aiming, threw the dagger and hit the center just where she had.

"Not better," Kat's voice came from behind them.

Even though Kat was on her side, Olivia was irked that she had arrived. Not that Olivia wanted to be alone with Henry.

Henry bowed to Kat. "Cousin, Kat. My congratulations to Michael on finding himself so fetching a princess. You have certainly grown to be a beautiful young woman."

Kat blushed. Something Olivia had never seen her do. "You're engaged?" Olivia asked, seeing her last cousin lined up to be a married woman and the end of the Perilous Princesses.

"Not yet," Kat said. "Someday. We have more important things to do before that." She lifted her eyebrows at Olivia.

"What would that be?" Henry had retrieved the dagger and held it out to Olivia.

"None of your business," Olivia snapped, taking the knife and wondering why she was so irritated.

"That was rude," Kat said, lifting her eyebrows at Olivia. She directed her gaze to Henry. "She's just upset because you throw as well as she does." Kat cocked her head to one side, and Olivia knew that head position. It meant Kat was up to something.

"Or was that just luck?" Kat asked.

Henry laughed. "I don't know. Shall we have a contest and see?"

Smiling, Kat said, "Let's. I'll throw too."

For the first time since they started The Perilous Princesses, Olivia did not want one of the members to participate. What was wrong with her? She shook it off and woke the Weaponry Master. "We need more daggers. Prince Henry will be throwing with us."

The groggy Weaponry Master managed to bring an armful of daggers back quickly. But not fast enough for Olivia. While he was gone, she listened to Henry and Kat banter. Olivia tamped down her irritation, which she absolutely knew was not jealousy.

Now looking at the carved dragon on the dagger

the Weaponry Master held, made her feel that dancing fire moving across her skin. Her brain twisted with thoughts of flying, of spitting fire, of being a dragon. Crazy thoughts. Crazy, but it felt like she was almost ... not all human. She had to find out if dragons were extinct or if the curse Kat awoke would really come and decimate them ... or if there was any way a human, maybe a princess, could become a dragon.

She had half-formed the perfect plan to get into the forbidden library room when Kat poked her in the side, and Henry snickered.

"Are we ready?" he asked. He took a dagger from the Weaponry Master and held it out to Olivia. "Shall I choose the target?"

She and Kat nodded. He looked around the courtyard. Finally he pointed to a carved wooden column. "The owl at the top. The center of his eye. First one to get closest."

The owl's eye was a smaller target than they usually practiced on, but Olivia was sure she could hit the mark. "You are the guest. You throw first."

He bowed, taking the dagger, lining it up, and squinting one eye. He threw and hit the owl's eye dead center.

Kat's breath hissed in. But Olivia would not give herself time to worry. She strode to the owl, retrieved the dagger and returned to stand where Henry had. Keeping both eyes open as the master had taught her, she threw straight and true. Her throw landed right where his had.

Kat followed but missed the eye. The three picked targets and threw over and over. Kat missed a few times, but Henry and Olivia did not. Olivia had to admit she was enjoying the contest. She forgot to worry about dragons until clapping broke out after her last throw sliced off exactly one small branch of the overgrown boxwood bush.

She looked around and found that her father, uncles, brothers, her sister, and Melinda had gathered. This was the first time Olivia's family, outside her sister and cousins, had attended her weaponry practice. She was not sure how to explain that Kat could throw so well, since only Olivia was supposed to be part of the lessons. But Kat's father clapped and grinned along with the rest.

Olivia relaxed. She'd make her father proud. She'd beat Henry.

Henry stood a single overblown rose in a vase on a

table at the other side of the courtyard. "The one who can slice off a single petal wins." He bowed and handed her the dagger.

Olivia was so happy with how it was all going, that she didn't hesitate. She threw her dagger, but as she did a dark shadow blew over her eyes. Something flew overhead. Something that whispered that word, "becoming." But when she looked, there was nothing.

Her dagger sliced through the air, but missed the rose by a caterpillar's hair. Striding to the table to retrieve the dagger, Olivia was less worried about losing than she was about the shadow. No one else had uttered a peep. Had she really seen the shape of a dragon pass close to her? There was nothing now.

She returned and handed the dagger to Henry without a word. He looked at her, his forehead wrinkled. His eyes went from hers to the sky and back to her. For a moment she thought he was going to say something, but instead he aimed and threw, slicing off the petal Olivia had missed.

The boys behind Olivia cheered and ran to thump him on the back.

Melinda, Lisette, and Kat crowded around Olivia, and told her she did so well. Olivia watched her father turn and leave the courtyard without a word to her. He merely said, "Men, we have a hunt to attend." All the males including Henry followed him.

Olivia thanked the Weaponry Master and went to her chambers. She changed to a tunic and leggings for the hike down the hidden passage to the library. She'd thought about it and was sure that she knew where a hidden door might open on the forbidden library room.

But before she could move the tapestry that covered the hidden passage's door in her chamber's wall, the tapestry flew aside and Kat, Melinda, and Lisette spilled out of the passage. They were all dressed in their armor.

"We have a map to Dragon Mountain," Lisette said. "That's where the treasure is. We're going while everybody else is on this hunt. Put on your armor so if anyone sees us, we won't be recognized." She held out the black armor.

Olivia's mood bounced from happy to sad and back. She was glad they still wanted to be the brave and adventurous Perilous Princesses, but she couldn't get rid of the feeling that the dragons were not dead, and the Princesses were headed into trouble they couldn't handle. But that was silly, wasn't it? She was just tired from the party and being snarky about her sister and cousin getting married someday soon.

Everyone knew dragons had died out years ago. Dead things couldn't hurt you. They most assuredly couldn't turn you into a dragon. The Dragon Mountain would be perfectly safe. That scroll was so old, it was from before they died. If dragons lived, there would be writings about them in the new books not just in the forbidden room of ancient scrolls and books.

The others helped her into her armor. Like for the tournament, getting into the black armor made her feel wonderful. They hurried to the stables, where Melinda and Lisette convinced the stable master they were guests who needed horses at once.

The four did not look like prosperous knights since they had no servants or banners, but they also did not look like princesses. When they rode past the hunting party, the hunters bowed to them and cheered. The hunters had recognized the four knights from the tournament. Oddly no one tried to stop them. And odder, Henry pointed at her and grinned.

Olivia ignored him. He was just trying to be more important than the other hunters.

The princesses were halfway to the mountain when

the ground began to shake. Their horses, not war horses but riding horses who should never have carried a knight in armor, reared and screamed. All four princesses were dumped off, and the beasts turned and ran back toward the castle.

"Well, that's going to make it a lot harder to get to the mountain and back," Olivia said struggling to her feet.

"If we live to make it back!" Kat yelled, looking upward. "Everybody have your weapons?"

Olivia and the others looked up too. A dragon, glistening in poison green scales, flew toward them. Oliviia's heart beat faster. So much for being extinct. She was a little glad that this time everybody else saw it too.

"How did it know we were coming?" Melinda pulled back her bow and aimed for the beast. But she did not shoot. Lisette and Kat pulled out their swords and stood beside Melinda.

"The curse," Olivia said as she looked at her dagger. Could she throw and hit the vulnerable spot on a dragon? Where was that?

The dragon circled and abruptly dropped to the road. It was the image of what a dragon summoned by a curse should look like: red beast eyes; flames dripping out of its mouth. It roared and charged at the four princesses.

And it happened again. Just like at the tournament, she heard the whispered *becoming* and felt her body changing. Fast this time, as fast as the dragon ran at them. She felt her arms stretch like wings, and her mouth grow hot. Flames dripped onto the road in front of her. A low growl ripped through her throat.

The dragon turned its head to her. It stared. For a moment she thought it would back off. But instead it roared and charged again. Melinda, Lisette, and Kat screamed and ran toward it, all three with swords drawn. Olivia was quicker. She flapped her wings and flew at the dragon, spitting a flame that tasted of the persimmons she had for breakfast and the anger she felt at this creature for threatening them.

Olivia and the dragon met in mid-air clawing at each other, spitting and dodging. Below them the princesses watched. Olivia matched the dragon attack for attack, but she could not win. The dragon kept fighting back. If she couldn't defeat it, they would all die.

She needed something more. Some way to kill it, or force it to fly away. Her breath came harder, and her wings felt like she was about to drop when Kat yelled from the ground, "Catch!"

Olivia kicked the dragon away and peeled into a glide that took her close to Kat. Somehow the tips of her wings worked like her hands, and she snatched the dagger in the air and turned back. The dragon was now only a wingspan away. For Olivia this was an easy toss, except the dragon cocked a wing to swoop away. Olivia beat her wings in one huge effort and crashed into the dragon. She grabbed him with her hind legs and plunged her dagger into the beast's chest.

It screamed.

Pain seared through Olivia's chest as if she was the one who had been stabbed. But she was not bleeding. It was the other dragon falling to the ground. She swept her wings back to fly away from its descent. But the dragon's wings tilted, and it swerved and headed back toward the mountain.

Olivia dropped to the road, gasping for breath. Her wings were gone. The princesses gathered around her. "You did it again! You were amazing!"

She looked at them. "You know what I turned into?"

"Well, duh," Kat said. "Same as at the troll attack. You turned into a whirling ball of energy."

"No." Olivia couldn't believe they didn't see her as a dragon. "I turned into a dragon."

"Don't be silly. You're not a dragon." Lisette brushed the hair back from Olivia's eyes. "How did you learn to be so fast and ... look like a flaming ball? You need to teach us," Lisette insisted.

"It's gone now. We still need the magic power stone. How are we going to get to the mountain and get it?" Kat asked.

Olivia and the others turned to her. "We aren't," Melinda said. "Not today. We aren't prepared. Right, Olivia?"

Olivia nodded. "There has to be more information in the library. We'll find out how to get the stone without getting ourselves killed."

Reluctantly Kat nodded, and they began the trek back to the castle. It was only minutes before they encountered Henry riding slowly toward them. The princesses were so hot and tired, none of them had on their helmets. Olivia tried to think of how to explain their armor and keep him from revealing who they were, but a moment later the whole hunting party came out of the woods at a canter.

"It's all over now," Olivia said. Her father would be

angry about her endangering them all, disobeying him by including the princesses in her lessons, and generally lying. She'd fess up and hope the punishment would not exceed her lifespan.

As the hunting party stopped their horses, Henry dismounted and walked over to her. "Black armor. Why am I not surprised you're that one?"

"Huh?" Olivia said and immediately regretted sounding so clueless.

Facing the other hunters, Henry said, "May I introduce the Perilous Four that saved the castle from the trolls."

Olivia's brother Ian laughed. "Right. Just because they dress up in armor like those knights, doesn't mean it's them."

Olivia's father held up a hand. "Is it true?"

The four princesses nodded.

"Can you prove it?" Ian asked.

Henry interrupted. "Well, I know Olivia has the dagger skills of the black knight."

Olivia's father shook his head and asked, "These princesses defeated the trolls?"

"And a dragon!" Kat said.

"Pardon?" Olivia's father said. The rest of the party

stared silently.

Kat held up a black scale Olivia was pretty sure had come off herself since it was the color of her armor and not green like the other dragon.

"We wanted to get the dragons' power stone to save the farmers' crops," Kat said. Olivia shut her eyes and wished Kat would stop talking. It was only getting worse.

Olivia's father gazed at each of them for what felt like forever. At last he turned his horse, and said over his shoulder, "I think princesses who spy on Council meetings had better attend them and contribute." He stopped his horse and turned back. "Give me the dragon's scale." It was handed to him, and he rode on.

Melinda was handed up to ride behind Bryand. Lisette was helped up onto Willum's horse, and Kat climbed up on Michael's. Only Olivia still stood in the road staring at the dust and trying to think of a way out of this trouble. She did not look up. She would not beg. A gloved hand reached down past her face and wiggled its fingers.

She peered through her golden bangs. Henry grinned at her. "Not flying home?"

She froze for a moment. Her ears had to still be full

of the dragon's roars. Henry couldn't have said what she thought she heard. She couldn't ask him. What would she say? She couldn't ask about becoming a dragon. It wasn't possible. He was making a joke.

She let him help her up on his horse.

"You have been very busy. It takes a lot of practice to be as good as you are," Henry said. "The others have trained along with you?"

"Yes." There was no point in hiding that truth any longer. "We call ourselves The Perilous Princesses." Who cared if he laughed?

But he didn't. "There's an old tale about a race of dragons who were more dangerous than any other. It's said they could morph, even making their wings into human hands. Hands that could hold daggers." He stopped for a moment then continued, "Aren't you the best princess at using a dagger?" He chuckled. "But then dragons don't exist, do they?"

For a moment, Olivia didn't answer, then she muttered, "They're extinct. Why are you talking about dragons?"

Henry turned and looked at her. "Becoming."

"What?" she demanded.

But he only laughed and ignored her question.

"Maybe I'd like to help the famers too. Maybe I'm just interested in dragons. I think you are too. It's nice to have common interests."

He stopped for what felt like forever before he went on in a serious tone, "I'm becoming very, very good with a dagger. Maybe dragon good."

They were both silent the rest of the ride home. Olivia spent the time thinking about where Henry had been these past years, about how he was a fostered prince, and how he was not like his brothers.

And how she was becoming very much not like her sister.

At seven years old **Kath Boyd Marsh** self-published her first fantasy on lined notebook paper starring a creature based on her little sister. Before Kath moved to Richmond, KY to write about dragons, wizards, and other fantastic creatures, she lived in seven states, Panama, and one very haunted house. T*he Lazy Dragon and the Bumblespells Wizard* was her debut novel. Visit her and the dragons at KathBoydMarshauthor.com.

So the Story Goes

Christine Marciniak

Once upon a time, a very long time ago when the countries we know now were no more than a patchwork of very small kingdoms, there lived a young man who wanted to be king. However, he was the youngest son of the youngest son. When he went to his grandfather and said he was ready for a kingdom, his grandfather, the King, told him he had no kingdom to bestow upon him, not even a fiefdom, for they had all gone to his uncles and brothers and cousins.

"You'll have to make your own way in the world," the King told him.

So, he did.

He crossed rivers and valley and mountains until he came to the cave of a dragon where a beautiful princess was being held captive. He proved his courage by challenging the dragon, he proved his strength by removing the rocks that trapped the princess, he proved his honor, by not taking the jewels the dragon guarded. For his reward the dragon promised his protection for a thousand years if he started *his kingdom right there.*

Oh, and he married the princess and they lived happily ever after as the first king and queen of Colsteinburg.

Tessa stirred the steaming cauldron with a large wooden spoon. The scent of vegetables and spices made her stomach gurgle. In the corner of the cave the big red dragon made a gurgling sound as well.

"It's almost ready, Cole," she assured her protector. "I need to make sure the potatoes are soft. You don't want to get an upset stomach from eating underdone potatoes."

"I never get an upset stomach," the dragon grumbled.

"That's because I am careful about what I feed you," Tessa said and brought the spoon up to her mouth to taste the broth.

"You're cheating, eating before it's ready."

Tessa laughed. "You big baby." She poked at a potato, decided it was soft enough and ladled some of the soup into a bowl for herself. Then she removed the cauldron from the fire and placed it in front of the dragon's large head. "There you go. Dinner is served."

"Are you sure the potatoes are done?" Cole asked,

looking at her through his double-lidded eyes.

"Absolutely certain," she said. She nestled herself in a pile of pillows and ate her bowl of soup while Cole stuck his face in the cauldron and slurped. He was licking the pot clean when he picked up his head and tilted his ears toward the entrance of the cave.

"Someone's coming," he said.

Tessa's shoulders tensed, and she prepared herself for what was likely to come. She hated when people found the cave and her. Was it a lone adventurer? Was it a knight out to slay a dragon and steal his treasure? Was it the people who killed her family?

"Should I go see?"

"Absolutely not. I cannot protect you if you are in front of me, instead of behind. Stay where you are." He lumbered to his feet and, careful that his swaying tail did not hit Tessa as he walked, he made his way to the entrance of the cave and looked out. "It is another young cavalier," he said. "Do you think he wants the treasure or the princess?"

The dragon chuckled to himself. He liked the challenge these men gave him.

"Perhaps both," Tessa said. They came with increasing regularity, these knights and adventurers. Some wanted to steal the treasure that everyone knew dragons guarded, others wanted to rescue the princess that they had heard was trapped in the cave.

"Maybe he will be worthy of you," Cole said, with what Tessa thought might be a tinge of hope in his voice.

"Tired of guarding me, are you?" she asked. The protection spell she had put on him would only lift when she found a man worthy of her. Based on the men who had made their way to the cave, she doubted that was ever going to happen.

"It's been three years," he said with the dragon-equivalent of a shrug.

Three years since her family was killed, the kingdom taken, and the only way she could keep herself safe was to run away and find protection where she could get it. Three years that she'd been living in a cave and tending her garden with her only companion a dragon.

But she never thought any man who came up this mountain was worthy. They were greedy and braggadocios and crude and violent. That was not the kind of man she wanted. Though, perhaps the kind of man she might like was not the kind to climb a mountain and challenge a dragon. She tried not to think about that. Besides, she didn't mind living in the cave. Cole was good company.

Tessa left her nest of soft pillows and sidled up next to Cole, placing one hand on the rough leather of his dragon skin. She peered through the opening of the cave to the young man making his way up the mountain. He had a walking staff in one hand and wore a tunic of leather with red wool tights. His hair was bright red, and he had a friendly, open face. He stopped and looked toward the cave, and his expression changed to one of consternation.

"He looks nice," Cole said encouragingly.

"You always think they look nice," Tessa answered. "You cannot judge by looks. The men who killed my parents were quite handsome."

"I do not always think they look nice," Cole contradicted. "Remember the one last month who had evil eyes and a nose that was too large. I did not like the looks of him."

That was true. There were times he didn't think they looked nice, but if Tessa had to guess she'd say that Cole didn't like being under the protection spell she'd put on him and wanted to be free. She had to be careful that he didn't push her to accept someone she didn't want.

Cole stuck his head out the cave and blew a stream of fire toward the traveler.

Tessa stifled a laugh as the startled young man nearly fell over. Would he turn and run? Some did when they realized that the dragon was real and they would be in danger if they approached. More often they unsheathed their swords and marched forward. This young man righted himself, straightened his jaunty felt hat and set his sights back up toward the cave.

"What are you trying to keep me from, dragon?" the man hollered up the hill.

Cole of course didn't answer him. Cole did not make it general practice to talk to everyone who approached his cave. Instead he breathed more fire.

"You really don't want me to come up there, do you?" the man responded, but instead of sounding put off, he sounded determined.

"Well, he's not easily frightened," Cole said to Tessa. "That makes him brave."

"Or foolish," Tessa answered.

The man was out of sight now, hidden by the rocks and crags of the mountainside.

"Get rid of him," Tessa said.

"Let him have a chance to prove his worth."

Tessa sighed. "He's not worthy. None of them are worthy."

"Let him try and fail if need be," Cole said. "But let him try."

"Fine, but it is up to me to determine if he is worthy," Tessa reminded Cole. She was not a pawn to be brokered by other people. She was the one to decide who would win her.

Cole grunted and together they settled in to wait until the man should come into sight again. Soon the feather in his hat was visible amid the scrub pines and wild flowers. Then his hat, and then the rest of him, came into view.

The man stopped abruptly when he caught sight of Tessa standing next to the dragon in the opening of the cave.

"I will rescue you," the man said, jutting his chin out with determination. "Stand back, and all will be well."

The same old story. They never even stopped to ask if she needed rescuing, just assuming that because she was female she must. Well, let him try. The protection spell was strong. He wouldn't get past the dragon. Very few did.

"Get back," Cole growled at her, and she obeyed, moving farther back into the cave, situating herself on her pillows again. Then with a wave of his tail, Cole scattered large rocks between her and the opening of the cave.

It was a standard test. If the adventurer did make it past Cole, would he have the strength to move the rocks that seemed to trap her? The strong ones could shift the rocks, the wily ones found their way around the rocks, but either way they often treated her as a prize they had earned. She was no one's prize.

She peered through the gaps in the rocks and watched the exchange between the new adventurer and Cole.

"You are holding a young woman prisoner," the man said.

"I am not," Cole answered.

The man didn't seem astonished that Cole spoke to him. Perhaps he had encountered dragons before.

"I saw her. You have a beautiful woman trapped in your cave."

Tessa rolled her eyes. A typical flatterer. They all thought she was beautiful. And while she certainly appreciated the sentiment, did being beautiful make her any more deserving of rescue? Or love, when it came to that. It did not.

"What do you propose to do about it?" the dragon asked.

"I cannot fight you," the man said. "You are much bigger, and I have no arms but my walking stick. I could perhaps outwit you and rescue her."

"Perhaps you could," Cole said. "But I am not easily outwitted."

"I thought not," the man said. "You are quite an intelligent dragon. Anyone can clearly see that."

This was a new approach, Tessa thought. Most men did not think to use flattery on the dragon. And she'd lived with Cole long enough to know that he was particularly susceptible to it.

Cole preened a little.

"A very handsome and large dragon," the man continued. "I have met other dragons, and you are by far the most formidable I've encountered."

"What happened when you met the other dragons?" Cole asked.

"One ate my horse," the man said. "Another melted my sword."

"And you think you can get past me? The strongest, most beautiful and most amazing dragon of all?" Cole asked.

Tessa had to put a hand over her mouth to stop herself from laughing. Cole was certainly the most conceited dragon anyway.

"Oh no!" the man said. "That clearly isn't possible. But I was wondering, how far can you breathe flames? The exhibition earlier was impressive, but I'm sure it was only a small demonstration. For example, could you set fire to that tree over there?"

Tessa couldn't see what tree he pointed to, but she watched Cole slowly move from the entrance of the cave so he could see the tree the man pointed to. And then with one quick breath he apparently did exactly what the man requested.

"Amazing!" the man said. "Absolutely amazing. And what about that one?"

Cole moved further out of the entrance to the cave and quick as a wink the man was past him and inside. She waited for the sound of him trying to move the rocks, instead his head appeared over the top of the rock fall. He'd simply climbed them, which made him one of the smarter ones. Soon he was behind the rocks with her.

She shrunk back against her pillows. Now was the big test. He may have thought the test was bypassing the rocks, but in reality the test was how he would treat her once he had.

"I am Frederick Mohr," the man said, sweeping his hat off and making a courtly bow at the waist. "Who do I have the pleasure of addressing?"

Such a dignified introduction deserved a dignified response.

"I'm Princess Teresa Elaina Bodenmuller," she answered. The kingdom had been overrun and the king and queen were dead, but she saw no reason to renounce her title. Often when the adventurers heard her title they became even more determined to remove her from the cave, regardless of what she wished. One time a man even had her over his shoulder and was attempting to carry her away. Cole had intervened at that point, plucking her from the man's back by snagging her dress in his large mouth and tripping the man so he tumbled down the mountain. He had not come back to try again. Unworthy.

"Are you a prisoner?" Frederick asked with proper deference. No one had ever asked before. They all assumed she must be. Why did he not make that assumption? Did he know other people who lived with dragons? She wanted to know more about this man and what had shaped his world view.

"I am not. I live here." She raised her chin in proud defiance, in case he had an issue to make with her living arrangements.

"Then you do not need my help to leave here, do you?" he said with remarkable perception.

"I do not," Tessa said, "but I appreciate the thought."

He sighed and leaned against the largest rock, crossing his arms in front of himself and looking thoroughly dejected.

"I'm not a very good adventurer," he admitted. "I thought perhaps my luck would change and I could rescue a damsel in distress, but I suppose first I'd have to find a damsel who truly was in distress."

Tessa grinned at him. She hated to admit it, but she liked him. He was so unlike the other men who came here full of bluff and bluster.

"Why are you adventuring? Why are you not safely at home?"

Again he sighed, but then he straightened up and said with determination and pride, "I am the youngest son of the youngest son of a king and there is no kingdom for me. I have set forth to find my own fortune."

"Dragon's caves often hide treasures," Tessa said,

testing his character. Would he try to steal it, proving himself unworthy of her attention?

He smiled, and she liked the way his cheeks dimpled. "I have found the treasure that his cave houses, and it is named Princess Teresa Elaina."

"Tessa," she said, a smile spreading across her face. "My friends call me Tessa." Even as she said it she chastised herself for letting her guard down. After all, he was a master of flattery. He had tricked Cole, and she could not let him trick her.

"Come out!" Cole bellowed from the other side of the rocks.

Frederick shot Tessa a panicked look.

She gave him her most benign smile. "You can't come into the dragon's inner sanctum and not expect repercussions."

He took a deep breath and squared his shoulders. "Will he expect me to fight him to the death?"

"Probably not," Tessa said. Fights to the death did happen occasionally. Always the adventurer's death, of course. Dragons were notoriously hard to kill. Why people continued trying constantly bemused her. More often the adventurer simply left, bloody and bruised and already creating the great story he would tell about his conquests when he got back home.

"What is it you want?" Frederick asked, his voice surprisingly stable.

"You must clear the rocks from the cave," Cole's voice was smug with self-satisfaction.

Frederick's eyebrows shot up and Tessa shrugged.

"Why?" Frederick answered. "You put them there."

Tessa laughed out loud, and she could just imagine the look on Cole's face for being stood up to like that.

"I put them there to keep you from Tessa," Cole answered.

"Didn't work," Frederick responded. Tessa couldn't believe what she was hearing. He was either a lot stupider or a lot braver than she had thought. And she didn't think he was stupid.

It was possible he was worthy though.

Time to continue testing him to find out.

"The rocks do need to be moved," Tessa said. "Cole cannot put them all back as easily as he can scatter them. I can help you if you'd like."

"You do not need to help," Frederick answered, "I can do it on my own."

Tessa shrugged and settled down into her pillows again. "Okay, fine," she said.

So, he had failed the test. Assuming she couldn't help simply because she was female. He'd find that it was much easier with two, especially since she had a long stick that made an effective lever for getting the rocks out of the way.

She had almost started wishing that he was the worthy one. She could almost imagine living with him and seeing that cheerful smile every day. But, there was no point in dreaming, just like all the others he had proven himself unworthy.

He crawled back over the rock fall and began to lift the rocks closest to the cave entrance. She could hear him grunting and struggling to shift the rocks. After a quarter of an hour he had moved one or two. She poked her head over the rock fall and watched him. He was red in the face and straining his muscles.

Cole was sitting in the entrance of the cave, watching with a self-satisfied gleam in his eye. He gave Frederick enough room to get past him, but offered no assistance.

"Are you sure you don't want help?" she asked, not at all sure why she was giving him a second chance.

"It would probably be easier with two," Frederick admitted, "but since it is my fault the rocks are here, it is my responsibility to move them."

Wait. That was the reason he didn't want help? Because it was his responsibility? Well, that was different. Maybe he was worthy after all. Suddenly the world seemed much brighter

"It is partly my fault," she admitted. "Cole has to protect me, and the rock fall is one way."

Frederick stopped struggling with a rock that was twice as big as his head.

"Do you know an easy way to move the rocks?" he asked. "Perhaps you have a magic spell or something?"

Tessa took a step back. "I am not a witch!" she said indignantly and retreated to her pillows.

A witch indeed! She'd only used a spell once, and she was surprised when it had worked. Clearly the protection spell on Cole had worked, but that did not make her a witch. Did it?

Soon his head popped up over the rocks. "I never said you were," he explained. "I thought that since you were offering you might have a plan, because if it were simply to share in backbreaking work, I think most people wouldn't bother to say anything."

"I'm not most people," Tessa said, feeling petulant.

"I figured that," Frederick answered. "You live with

a dragon. That's fairly unusual." The looked at each other for a long second. Finally Frederick asked again. "So, do you have an easy way?"

He was asking for her help. He was admitting he could use her help. That gave him lots of positive points as far as she was concerned. She nodded. "I do," she said. "I'll help."

She climbed back over the rock fall, ignoring the gimlet gaze of Cole sitting in the entrance. She found the long stick she used as a lever and showed Frederick how propping the stick against one rock and nudging the next got the rocks to move. She let him use the lever while she moved some of the smaller rocks herself.

"You could help, you know," she said to Cole as she passed out of the entrance to the cave.

"I much prefer watching," Cole said in a self-satisfied way.

"Of course you do," Tessa answered with a roll of her eyes.

It was full dark before the rocks had all been moved out of the cave and Frederick looked near tired to death. She found her jug full of mead and offered it to him. "I think you've earned a drink" she said.

He took a grateful draw.

"Thank you." He handed the jug back to her. "I suppose I should be on my way."

"I suppose you should stay here for the night where it is safe. You don't know what you might encounter out there."

"No, but there's a dragon in here who doesn't like me that much."

"Cole? He likes you."

Cole grunted in what may have been disagreement.

"Well, regardless, this is my cave and I say you may stay the night. I have some bread to offer you and a blanket to cover yourself with for the night."

Again he smiled in a way that showed his dimples. "Your cave? Not the dragon's?"

"We share it," Tessa said. That was all the explanation he needed. It was her cave as much as it was Cole's. They were both destined to live here together, protector and protectee, until she deemed some man worthy to share her life with. She was beginning to wonder if perhaps that man was in front of her. Of course, there was one test left, and he would encounter that in the morning.

She fed Frederick and offered him a soft pillow and a warm blanket and showed him a place he could sleep.

Cole moved from the entrance of the cave to position himself between Tessa and Frederick as they settled in for the night. The protector took his job seriously.

In the morning when she awoke, Frederick was already up and poking at the fire. He had gone out to the spring and filled the coffee pot and the smell of percolating coffee filled the cave. It was almost decadently luxurious to not have to do that herself.

"I'm not sure where you keep the cups," he said when he saw her.

"Actually, we only have the one," she said. "Cole doesn't use a cup to drink, and I don't often have guests."

"Can't imagine why not," Frederick said. He stretched his back.

"Sore?" she asked.

"A bit. But it was nice to have a warm blanket for the night. Thank you."

"You have the first cup of coffee," she said. "You made it. You deserve it."

He didn't argue, but poured the coffee into the cup she offered him. "We could share," he said.

"I'll have a cup when you are done."

"Perhaps we can sit outside the cave and watch the sun come up," Frederick said. "I love watching the way the mountains change as the light changes."

Behind her Cole snorted, but Tessa ignored him. She and Frederick sat on large rocks outside the cave entrance. It was fascinating to watch as the colors emerged in the scrub pines and the flowers as the sun made its way across the sky.

"Where are you off to next?" Tessa asked.

"I don't know. I will keep going until I find a likely kingdom, I suppose."

"And what would that look like?" Tessa asked. "I mean, I don't suppose there's just some castle somewhere waiting for you to move in and take over."

"No, I suppose that's not what I would find," he admitted. "I don't really know. I kind of figured I would know it when I saw it."

"A treasure would make it easier, perhaps," Tessa said, baiting him. "You could buy a castle that someone didn't want anymore."

"A treasure like the one in the cave?"

So, he had seen it.

"Yes, like that one. You are smart and could probably figure out a way to get Cole out of the cave again so you could take it."

Frederick gazed back into the cave again and

sighed. "I might be able to, it's true. But I could not start my life on stolen treasure. It wouldn't be right. I wouldn't respect myself, and I suspect you wouldn't respect me much either."

"Does it matter if I respect you?" she asked.

"It matters very much," he said. "Because when I have found my kingdom, I plan to come back here and find you and see if you are ready to leave the cave and live in my kingdom with me."

From inside the cave Cole roared and Tessa and Frederick jumped.

"Did I make him angry again?" Frederick asked.

"I don't think so," Tessa said, but she couldn't imagine what the problem was. She got up and went to Cole's side. His head was resting on his front paws, and a giant tear was traveling from his eye, down past his nose, and about to drop into the dirt floor of the cave.

"Whatever is wrong, Cole?" she asked him. "Frederick has been completely honorable. Why are you sad?"

"Because he is worthy. I know he is worthy and so do you. And you will leave me."

"Where will I go?" Tessa asked, putting a soothing hand on the dragon's large head. "He has no kingdom,

So the Story Goes 139

and he says he will come back for me when he does. That could be years."

"Do you think he is worthy?" Cole asked pointedly.

Tessa took a deep breath, and looked out to where Frederick was still sitting, enjoying his coffee and the morning sun. He had proven himself worthy at every step. If there was anyone who she would leave the cave for, it was him, but he wasn't asking her to go anywhere yet. "He's worthy," she admitted.

"Then he will have his kingdom," Cole said. The dragon sniffed once and the tears stopped. He lumbered toward the opening of the cave.

"Frederick Mohr, youngest son of the youngest son of a king," Cole said, proving he'd been listening to their conversation earlier. "You have been deemed worthy by Princess Tessa. Because of this, the treasure that I safeguard is yours."

Frederick jumped up, nearly spilling his coffee. "You mean, that I am worthy of Tessa? For she is surely the treasure you mean. But I cannot take her if she does not wish it."

"I wish it," Tessa said, coming up beside him.

"There is another treasure," Cole said. "You uncovered it when moving the rocks. You were even tempted to take a jewel or two, I saw you hold one and weigh it and wonder, but you put it back. You are an honest man. The treasure is now yours, and you can build you kingdom. Build it here, by my mountain, and I will offer my protection for the next thousand years."

Frederick put the coffee cup down on the rock he'd been sitting on and took Tessa's hands in his. "Will you be my wife?" he asked, looking deep into her eyes.

Her face hurt from smiling. "I will," she said. She had often dreamed of this day, but even in her dreams she had never imagined being this happy.

"Will you be my queen and help me run our kingdom?"

"I will," she answered, and then with a sideways glance at her dragon, she added. "As long as we name it after Cole. It shall be the kingdom of Colsteinburg."

And so it was.

Christine Marciniak was born in Philadelphia, but has spent most of her life in New Jersey. She has written several books for middle grade, young adults, and adults and hopes to write many more.

The Princess and the P

Steve DuBois

Mynda threw open the door and rushed into the king's bedchamber. "Oh, Father, I'm so uncomfortable!" she cried. "I tossed and turned and didn't sleep a wink all night!"

Caedmon, the venerable King of Lexico, sat up slowly, satin sheets sliding aside to reveal velvet pajamas. "What is it, my angel?" he yawned. His eyes were full of sleep but empty of surprise; the seventeen-year-old princess was widely renowned for her sensitivities, and the path between the royal bedchambers was well-worn with footsteps from her midnight tirades.

"It's the P, Father!" she exclaimed. "I can't sleep because of the P!"

The king nodded. "A rubber sheet, then," he said. "I shall instruct your chambermaids to …"

"No, not that! The *letter* P!" Mynda rushed to his bedside. "P is the source of all our kingdom's misfortunes!" She sat beside him on the goose-down mattress. "Is it not true, Father, that the words we speak shape the reality in which we live?"

The king nodded. "In some respects. Discourse has power. The way in which we talk about people and things influences the way in which we interact with them. A mighty lord who refers to his serfs as 'dogs' will come to see them as less than human, and he will treat them less kindly than one who speaks of them as 'my people.' A knight who demeans his squire by calling him 'boy' will raise up a less mighty warrior than one who calls his squire by name." He paused. "And it is true that here in the glorious Kingdom of Lexico, words have even more power than they do elsewhere."

The princess nodded vigorously. "And what element is common to all the crises that beset our loyal subjects, Father?"

The royal brow furrowed. "I suppose … money?"

"No, Father. Think harder."

"Alcohol?"

"No."

"Millennials?"

Mynda gritted her teeth, and reached into her dressing gown to withdraw a vellum scroll. "Behold, Father," she said, unrolling the scroll. "The source of our misery."

The king withdrew a pair of gold-rimmed spectacles from his bedside table, and squinted at the words. "Pestilence," he read. "Plague. Prostitution." He paused. "Patriarchy?"

"Oh, yes! I am so tired of the world being run by old white men who set arbitrary rules!"

The king blinked a bit at that, then continued. "Poverty, pneumonia, pets in restaurants …" He set the scroll down. "I perceive your point."

"It is the Ps, Father! The Ps oppress us!" Mynda's crystal blue eyes were furious. She took her father's hands. "Let us use the power granted us, Father! Instruct the royal wizards of Lexico to unleash their wordsmithing energy to police our language! Let every P be stricken and removed, that our people may prosper in the paucity of their plotting! May a purge become your urge!"

The king frowned and thought. At length, he replied, "Alas, Beloved, I dare not."

"But Father!"

Caedmon raised a finger. "'But' me no 'buts', my sweet." He shook his head, causing his glasses to skip askew. "This sort of thing has been attempted before. Even applied sparingly, word-magic is dangerous. It rends at the fabric of reality itself. A change of such magnitude as you suggest ... There is no foreseeing the risks." He shook his head again. "No, my dumpling. I dare not."

Mynda's cheeks went scarlet, and her crystal-blue eyes filled with tears of outrage. "But...but FATHER!"

Caedmon's face grew stern. "I dislike these buts, and I cannot lie," he intoned. "This old white man has spoken, Daughter. In time, you will come to see the wisdom of restraint. In the meantime ..." He flicked his fingers in a shoo-ing gesture. "To bed with you, girl. You will rule this kingdom in time. But not tonight."

Mynda scowled in fury and stalked away, slamming the door behind her. The old king sat upright for some time, moonlight streaming through the window. He knew his daughter well, and above all, he knew how relentless she could be when possessed by the spirit of justice. He squirmed in discomfort, first at the possibilities, and then for other reasons.

"Prostate," he muttered. "Yet another oppressive P word. It seems a minor purge is necessary after all." He reached for the royal chamber pot.

Beneath a cloak of dark green atop a dappled grey pony, Mynda rode in the moonlight down the dirt track that led deep into the forest where the word-witch waited. The going was rough, for the path was narrow and overgrown with brambles and bestrewn with aluminum cans and discarded candy wrappers. Nevertheless, she persisted, and at length she came upon the witch's cottage—a tiny, ramshackle structure in the middle of a small clearing, crudely constructed of pine, corrugated tin, and gingerbread.

An old woman stood on the front stoop, as if in anticipation of Mynda's arrival. The woman's face was lined and weathered, her skin tinged with green, but her eyes were bright and young. As they stared up at her, Mynda felt them pierce her soul. "A visitor!" the hag cried, trying, and failing, to convey a sense of surprise. "What would you have of me, young lady?"

"I have come for your help, crone," Mynda replied.

The word-witch nodded. "A crone, yes. A helper? No. Know this, traveler: *for magic, or for sage advice, all who come here must pay the price.*" She intoned the words with ritual solemnity. "An ancient formula, and I am bound to follow it to the letter. The magic of language comes dear indeed, and in exchange for it, you must give up something precious to you … Princess."

Mynda's eyes went wide. "You know who I am?"

"How not?" replied the crone. "Nothing is hidden from the gaze of a cunning woman. The way you sit sidesaddle, with perfect carriage, bespeaks years of training in horsemanship. Your bearing, erect and regal—the bent back of a peasant could never straighten so." She placed a finger to her chin, pondering. "Also, there's that diamond-studded tiara you're wearing. The subtle clues pile up." She beckoned with a crooked finger. Mynda dismounted and followed the old woman through a decaying oaken door into the tiny shack.

The word-witch led Mynda through the vestibule and down a long hallway into an antechamber, where she reached into a narrow barrel to withdraw a blood-red fruit. "Apple?" Mynda shook her head, and the witch grimaced. "Ah, well. Worth a try." They turned left through the conservatory, where an ornate harp plucked and strummed at itself and a sad-eyed monkey flitted hither and thither, its wings cramped behind the bars of a gilded birdcage, and stepped into the parlor. The word-witch rested her old bones on an elaborately upholstered divan. "What would you have of me, Highness?"

"The Ps, madam," Mynda said, her mouth a thin hard line. "I would have you round up every P in

Lexico. Gather them together, and do with them I care not what. But rid us of them!"

The word-witch nodded slowly. "A difficult letter, the P," she said. "One must mind them, as well as the Qs. An understandable concern. But this is no small task that you ask of me. *For magic, or for sage advice, all who come here must pay the price.* An ancient formula, and I am bound to every letter. The price for this will, I think, be quite high."

From her birth onwards, for seventeen full years, Mynda had been spoken to with only the greatest kindness and courtesy. As with everything else in Lexico, the words had shaped her. And she was, in truth, a touch spoiled by them; she had grown into a haughty young woman with a will like a rod of castle-forged steel. But the words had shaped her in other ways, too; she was made in the image of the compassion and courtesy she had always been shown. And as she thought upon the plight of her subjects—of their pain, of their panic, of their peanut allergies, of their every peril and peccadillo, her heart swelled with pity. She would do what was necessary. "I will pay."

The witch smiled, slowly and toothlessly. "A kidney, I think."

Mynda stared. "A *kidney*?"

The witch nodded. "As I said, I get few visitors out here, and one gets ever so hungry over the years. One grows tired of forest roots and lentils. A bit of protein in my diet would do me good."

Mynda's lovely countenance screwed up in revulsion. Still, her duty to her subjects was plain. She nodded.

The witch offered another toothless grin. She rose from the couch and beckoned with her crooked finger, leading Mynda down another long corridor, through the kitchens and dining room, past the scullery, through the Room Of Unspeakable Objects In Jars, and into a small workshop which held a single loom. The strings of the device appeared to be composed of paper, or perhaps parchment. Viewed straight on, they looked like threads, but when Mynda tilted her head it seemed to her that the paper *extended*, somehow, in a direction that was neither up nor down nor left nor right, a direction that made her brain squirm. She quickly gave up thinking about it. Seeing her discomfort, the word-witch cackled. "They call them *warps* for a reason, Highness."

The word-witch sat on a stool before the device

and took in her hand a shuttle which was, to all outwards appearances, a pen. "This will take a little while, Highness," she said and then went to work. Her hands were aged and liver-spotted, her fingers gnarled. Yet they flittered and flew with the speed and precision of hummingbirds, with a motion that was half-weaving and half-writing. As they did, it seemed to Mynda that she could feel a change; it was all around her, a subtle shift, like the smell of incipient thunder. And it was only a little while, not a lot of while, before the word-witch stood up from her stool. "It is done, Highness," she said. "When the sun rises in the morning, the change will be achieved." She extended her hand. "The payment, please."

Mynda was, in truth, quite fond of her kidneys, and had only recently had them redecorated. Still, a bargain was a bargain. With the greatest of reluctance, she chose the one of which she was less fond—the left—and placed it in the words-witch's waiting palm, where it squirmed and writhed a bit. And then, without another word, Mynda turned and strode with hasty steps down the many corridors and out the door into the night, where her steed waited to carry her back to the palace.

The sun shone in through the window of Mynda's bedchamber. Slowly she o*ened her eyes and blinked. *Was it all a dream?*

She rose from her featherbed and shuffled across the stone floor to her looking-glass. Her oval face stared back at her, eyes a bit reddened by her long night, but without any other a**arent change.

She wet her li*s, then o*ened her mouth to s*eak. "*ersimmon," she intoned. She blinked in sur*rise. "*achyderm." A slow smile cre*t across her face. "*eter *i*er *icked a *eck of *ickled *e**ers." She beamed. "It worked!"

Mynda couldn't wait to tell her father the good news. *Oh, he'll be cross at first, the old fuddy-duddy, but surely when he sees the *ositive changes I've wrought, he'll come around. Why, he'll be *leased as *unch!* She flung o*en the door which led to the flower garden that se*arated her chambers from the *alace itself.

She took one look at the garden, and her hands flew to her mouth. Her smile was re*laced by an ex*ression of outrage, and she hurled herself forwards through what was left of the garden and *ast the *ortcullis into the *alace's receiving room. "Father!" she exclaimed. "Father, my flowers have been ..."

She skidded to a sto*. The whole chamber was in

an u*roar. Her father sat u*on the throne with his head in his hands; ministers raced in and out relaying bits of news. In a corner sat her younger brother Caldwyn, infamous already at court for his vanity. He had what a**eared to be a *iece of ornamental statuary growing from the crown of his head, yet his ex*ression was one of de*ression and bewilderment rather than of *ain.

Worst of all was the sight in the middle of the chamber. At the center of the vortex stood the distinguished figure of Lady *riscilla, her father's ever-ca*able Lord Chancellor. She wore the chain of office about her neck and was unchanged in every res*ect save one: her head was missing. There was no blood or gore; there was sim*ly a body, a neck, and nothing above it.

"It is exactly as I feared, Majesty." Lady *riscilla s*oke, her tone measured and her voice clearly audible, even as it seemed to be issuing forth from nowhere. "Re*orts are flooding in from the outer *rovinces as we s*eak, and the situation is identical throughout Lexico. Two in every ten citizens have sim*ly vanished overnight, and everyone who's left seems to have a s*eech im*ediment."

She's remarkably calm, Mynda thought. *Father always said she was good at kee*ing her head.*

The old king, by contrast, was a quivering wreck. "But, how? Why?"

"As best we can tell, Majesty, the removal of a letter of our al*habet has wrought changes u*on the reality which that al*habet codifies. Wherever the letter has gone missing, reality has shifted accordingly. Hence: the immediate loss of two tenths of the kingdom's *o*ulation, including an eighth of the *easants, who do all the actual work."

Her father saw Mynda for the first time and rounded on her, his eyes flashing rare anger. "Oh, my child, my child!" he exclaimed. "What have you done?"

Mynda's head whirled. She knew not what to say. "My ... my flowers," she babbled.

The headless chancellor turned towards her. "The flowers of your garden, Highness? I *resume the daffodils and violets are unaltered?"

Mynda nodded numbly. "Yes. But the *etunias and the *eonies. They're ..."

"Missing their buds. Reduced to stems." It seemed to Mynda that Lady *riscilla might have nodded, but under the circumstances it was hard to be sure. "Wherever the missing letter a**eared at the beginning of a word, the to* of the object in question has gone missing. In those cases and all others, the object in question has been shortened in *ro*ortion to the amount by which its name has been shortened. I sym*athize with the loss of your flowers, Highness, but believe me," Lady *riscilla gestured to the em*ty s*ace at the to* of her neck, "others have it worse."

"Indeed," said a man-at-arms guarding the door. He, and every other male in the chamber, shared embarrassed glances with one another, then turned their combined glares on Mynda.

"But," Mynda stammered. "But I never."

"Lady *riscilla!" shouted the Mistress of Laws, scam*ering in through the far door. "We have confirmation! Crime is ram*ant throughout the ca*ital! The *olice force has been decimated!"

"To decimate something, Lady Hawley, is to reduce it by a tenth."

"Se*timated, then!"

"The harvest!" interjected the Minister of Agriculture. "A full fifth of the cro*s have disa**eared from the fields! More, in some cases! A full third of all the *eas! And with fewer *eons to harvest what remains, the kingdom will surely starve come winter!"

Mynda felt sick, and her disquiet was in no way

assuaged by the sight of her miserable brother with the statue—*an artistic nude*, she noted, *and actually quite well-crafted*—sticking out of his head. "Caldwyn," she moaned. "What have I done to you?"

Caldwyn, redolent of shame and reeking as always of mass-market body s*ray, looked u* at her with the dazed ex*ression for which he was, unfortunately, well known. "I…I was just combing my hair. Like I do every morning. And when I tried to *art it," he gestured at the statue, "this *thing* suddenly a**eared."

"This is the worst sym*tom of all, highness," Lady *riscilla said. "Some realities have been abbreviated by the elimination of the letter. Others have been *altered*. For when words transform into other words …"

The Minister of Agriculture broke in. "Our fruit orchards are in even worse sha*e than our fields," he grumbled. "The fruit is gone from the branches. Instead, half of the trees are full of ale, and the other half are full of ears. As a result, half the workers are too horrified to work, and the other half are too drunk."

The Marshall, res*lendent in his ceremonial armor, stood u* to s*eak. "We have received word that the narrow mountain *ass connecting our kingdom to Slibola has," he swallowed, "has been transformed, somehow, into a gigantic," he reddened, "into a gigantic *air of buttocks."

The Castellan s*oke. "I've just been to the city center," he said. "The *ublic *ark is now a huge wooden boat."

The King's *hysician interjected. "Our doctors cannot administer *ills to their *atients. The medicine itself makes them ill."

Lady *riscilla turned to Mynda. "Were flowers your concern, Highness? Come have a look at the state of your father's library." The headless chancellor strode across the chamber to the westernmost door and flung it o*en. Mynda crowded in behind her, and gas*ed in sur*ise. The shelves holding volumes of *oetry had shrunk by a sixth; all the other books were gone. In the s*ace where each tome had been, there was now a single rose.

The Chancellor was—*had been*—a formidably tall woman. She turned to face Mynda, who ex*erienced the unique sensation of being glowered down at by nothing whatsoever.

"It occurs to me, Highness," the Chancellor ruminated, her tone acidic, "that had you been 'with child' at the time this occurred, you would now be *regnant* ... which is to say, a ruling queen. Was that your intention? Was this an attem*t at a cou*?"

Mynda's eyes went wide with horror. "I...NO!" she exclaimed. "I would NEVER do that to Father! I just, I just wanted to *hel** the goodfolk of Lexico..."

"And indeed you have. They are in hell."

Mynda's mind raced. She glanced at the library full of roses, at the madness in the audience chamber, at the artwork in the center of her brother's hairstyle. And she thought about what the word-witch had said to her.

An ancient formula...

Slowly, an idea began to congeal in her mind.

"I can ... I can make this right." She nodded to herself. *Yes. It could work. But I'll need the right su**lies.* "I'll need ... I'll need some goods from the *alace kitchens. And a wand. From one of our word-wizards."

"A wand?" the king exclaimed. "You are a royal! You are untrained in the ways of sorcery."

"I won't need to be," Mynda re*lied. She thought, then nodded. *Yes. It could work.* "Trust me, everyone," she said. "I have a *lan."

A tri* to the royal stables *roved demoralizing, as Mynda discovered her *ony to be u*right, healthy, and headless. There was no question of attem*ting to ride

The *rincess and the * 157

him into the forest. Fortunately, the *alace's ornamental fish *ond was suddenly full of automobiles, so it was sim*ly a matter of towing them out, finding one whose engine still ran—a corroded but functional Buick—and hitting the road.

When Mynda's vehicle arrived in the clearing beside the word-witch's shack, the air was abuzz with ca*tured letters. They swarmed everywhere, their sad little tails dangling behind them, busy with yardwork and gardening, or *icking at windblown garbage with trash-s*ikes. The witch's home had gone neglected for decades, *erha*s centuries, and it seemed she was forcing her new em*loyees to make u* for lost time.

The crone herself was reclining on a lawn chair, sucking a tall cool glass of infant's blood through a straw, and regarded Mynda's oncoming Buick with an arched eyebrow. Mynda *ulled the car to a sto* then emerged. "Madam," she said, "I have come once again to bargain, and to liberate these consonants from their confinement."

The word-witch re*lied with a smirk and a dismissive wave. "I think not, my dialytic damsel. I am well-fed at this stage, and you cannot in any case com*ensate me again and ho*e to survive. Besides which, I have come to enjoy observing the efforts of my new labor force." She turned her gaze to the garden gate, where a row of *losive consonants were sweating in the hot sun, whitewashing a *icket fence, beside which stood a single *ink *lastic flamingo.

"Come now, madam. Remember the creed that governs you. Here is a customer before you. Let us strike a deal."

Another lackluster wave. "Go home. I have mastered the magic of words, and I find yours tedious."

"Very well," said Mynda. "I came to buy, but if you will not bargain with me, I shall liberate these letters by force." She reached into the car through the *assenger-side window and withdrew a thin wand of *olished ivory, which she *roceeded to *oint at the crone.

The old woman burst out laughing. "You fool of a girl! You cannot be serious! I have dueled the mightiest masters of linguistic magic! Satyrs, demons, and lawyers have fallen before me by the score. You cannot ho*e to best me!"

Mynda's blue eyes were icy cold as she *ointed the wand. "En garde, madam," she warned.

The word-witch rolled her eyes. "Oh, very well," she sighed. "We'll have this over with in a jiffy." She nodded to a gaggle of letters who were busy *atching a hole in the roof. "You there! Go inside and get the cauldron on the boil! I'll want sage, cloves, and onions from the *antry. In truth, I've develo*ed a taste for this one, and I antici*ate a royal feast tonight." The letters *araded reluctantly down off of the roof, then inside in a single-file line.

The word-witch *icked u* a small fallen willow branch from the shade of a nearby tree. She glanced at it and shrugged, muttered "Good enough," and then *ointed it ha*hazardly in Mynda's direction. "Are you sure you want this, girl?"

Mynda gazed down the length of the wand at her. "I renew my offer to buy."

The crone merely shook her head and stretched out her arm towards Mynda. She reached inside her mind, down and down, dee* inside, to the dark fathoms of vocabulary, where dictionaries dare not go and where lexicogra*hers fear to tread. And there she found the *erfect word, yes, a word uns*oken for millennia, eldritch and chthonic and ri*e with malice. She rolled it in her mouth, savoring it like wine; then she inhaled carefully so as not to suck any of it into her lungs, and sent it rumbling forth, like frozen breath on an icy morning.

It resounded with sorcerous *ower, withering the leaves on the trees that bordered the clearing, blackening the very air itself.

When the echoes faded, both women still stood, facing one another. The word-witch stared quizzically at Mynda, who grinned and lowered her wand.

"Still alive? Impossible," the word-witch muttered. Then, hearing the word emerge unaltered from her lips, and seeing the letters suddenly swarming out of the shack and in from all parts of the yard, her eyes went wide. "What ... what have you done?" The Ps surrounded Mynda, popping and prancing with new-found freedom, capering and cavorting in a widening celebratory circle.

Mynda smiled at her. "Why, I offered to buy. And you responded with a ..."

"A spell!" the word-witch replied. "A fatal spell! A word of sure and certain power ..." And then, the realization hit her. "A s— " She ground to a halt.

"Not a spell, under the circumstances. Rather: a *sell*," said the princess. "It was a pleasure doing business with you." The Buick was filling up with a plentitude of Ps; already they occupied every square inch of the backseat, as if a hippopotamus had eaten a hundred gallons of alphabet soup and then had an unfortunate accident on the upholstery.

But this time it was the word-witch's turn to smile. "Oh, but Highness, aren't you forgetting something? We made an *exchange*." Her toothless grin trailed a string of eager drool. "A legally and magically binding contract. You owe me a kidney—and it is a debt you cannot pay without forfeiting your life. I may be, suddenly, an unlettered woman, but still, I shall dine tonight. And not just upon a single kidney, oh no indeed." The word-witch smiled a smile as wide as all the world's sin.

Mynda nodded, her face impassive. "We did have a deal. And I shall pay you all that I owe." She walked around the car to the driver's side and withdrew a small burlap bag from below the seat. Tossing it to the crone, she slid in behind the wheel.

The word-witch undid the twine which held the bag closed, opened it, and found herself staring down at an abundance of small white grains. "This isn't a kidney. This isn't even meat." She glanced up in irritation. "What, do I look *vegan* to you?"

Mynda leaned her head out the window. "I believe you once told me you worked under an ancient formula," she said, "which you must follow to the letter. *To the letter.* And our deal was made under unique phonetic conditions, madam." The last of the Ps had made their way into the vehicle. Mynda turned the key in the ignition, heard the engine roar, and turned back to the word-witch one final time. "Speak, if you wish, the words of your ancient creed. The words you spoke when we made our deal. And then tell me what I owe."

"For magic, or for sage advice, all who come here must pay the ..." The witch did a double take, looked down at the bag of rice at her feet, threw back her head, and emitted a howl of feral rage.

She raised her wand to smite the princess. But Mynda was already gone, her taillights vanishing into the darkness, trailing Ps behind her like an overhydrated toddler.

In truth, things in Lexico never did get completely back to normal. A few Ps decided that they enjoyed the heady taste of freedom, and rather than returning to their assumed roles, they took to the open road, taking up life as hitchhikers, highwaymen, troubadours, and rogues. And so, every now and then, a blank space would turn up where a P was needed, and a suffering typesetter or jurist would shake his or her fist in the direction of the capital, cursing what had become known as Mynda's Mistake.

But the worst of the crisis had passed. The missing citizens returned, glad of the brief holiday, as did the crops and missing appendages. Lady Priscilla was particularly grateful and impressed by Mynda's cunning; her brother once again felt comfortable hitting the clubs on Saturday night, and her ever-affectionate father was quick to forgive her. And when, years later, Mynda finally came into her kingdom, she ruled with both compassion and wisdom—recognizing the power of words, but rarely seeking to police them. She opted instead to directly address the problems they described.

Neither the problems nor the problematic language were ever fully eradicated. Nevertheless, all involved lived more-or-less ha**ily ever after.

Steve DuBois is a high school teacher from Kansas City and the author of over a dozen professionally published short stories. For more of his work, visit www.stevedubois.net.

Aurora in the Dreaming

Alison Ching

In the castle behind the enchanted wood, Princess Aurora lay dreaming in the sleep of a hundred years. And in her dreaming, she walked.

She walked through time, a spectator of the scenes of her life that had shaped her fate. Of course, there was Lilac, her savior, telling her parents about the spell that would imprison her in sleep rather than death, but there were other moments, too: her mother weeping, a pile of burning spinning wheels, an ancient fairy dressed in darkest blue leaning over the cradle to seal Aurora's destiny.

She returned to this moment again and again, thinking that maybe if she watched it enough, it would make sense to her. That she could understand why the fairy Indigo would be willing to kill an innocent child.

It didn't work, though; Aurora never got an answer. That is, until the time she watched the scene unfold before her yet again—and looked up to see

Indigo watching her back.

Aurora gasped.

"You can see me?" she breathed, and Indigo laughed a bright, mad laugh.

"Of course, I can," she sang. "This is the dreaming, and the dreaming makes its rules to suit. It wanted us to meet, wanted us to speak. Maybe wanted you to ask a question."

Aurora trembled with wanting to know the answer and not wanting to know it.

"Why did you do it?" she whispered. "Why did you wish me dead?"

Indigo looked at Aurora with sad eyes, taking the princess's face in her hands.

"My darling," she said. "I did it to set you free."

And in a twist of starlight and flame, she disappeared.

In the dreaming, Aurora walked through space and found a flawless duplicate of the castle where her body lay in the waking world. She made her way through the still corridors, eerie in their silence, until she reached the great hall.

The hall was filled with slumbering people. They were dressed in servants' livery and military uniforms, velvet cloaks and sumptuous gowns. Some were stretched out on the floor or propped against the wall; others sagged forward with their heads on the tables next to lavish platters of food. Aurora walked among them, gazing at their faces. She had mostly been raised away from court, for her protection, so she recognized some of those she saw, but she found many of them strange.

What's happened to them? she wondered in distress. *Why are they here?*

Her parents were nowhere to be found, but that was not unusual; they often lived apart from her. It did feel strange and somewhat frightening, though, to be without her usual crowd of tutors and attendants telling her where to go, what to do.

Eventually, she made her way to the front of the hall, where the royal family traditionally sat during feasts, and found Sir Edgar, the captain of her father's guard, asleep on the edge of the dais. He was as still as the others, eyes closed and breath coming slow and deep.

With a trembling hand, Aurora reached out and touched Sir Edgar's arm.

In an instant, he snapped awake, throwing himself upright and looking around the room in alarm. When he saw Aurora, he dropped to one knee, his eyes on the floor.

"Your Highness," he said somberly.

"What is happening here?" she asked. "Who are all these people?"

"They came to celebrate your birthday, Your Highness," he said, still not meeting her eyes. "That is, until we heard about you …" Finally, he looked up at her, his brow furrowed in confusion. "They said you pricked your finger. That you had fallen into the magical sleep."

"I did," said Aurora.

"But then, how are you here talking to me?" Sir Edgar asked.

Rather than answer, Aurora turned and gazed out at the hall spread before them. Sir Edgar got to his feet and stood beside her, taking in the scene.

"Is this … are we in your dream?"

"Yes," Aurora said quietly.

"But … how?"

"I don't know."

After a long pause, Sir Edgar said, "We should wake the others."

"I suppose so," said Aurora.

And they stepped off the dais, into the thick of

the dormant bodies. Circling the room, Aurora woke each of the sleepers with a touch: Phillip, the page boy. Lord Dorian, her father's most senior councilor. Lady Adeline, the nursemaid from Aurora's early childhood. Polly, the assistant cook who made Aurora's favorite sweets. And so many others, including the ones Aurora had never met, who had traveled from far and wide to reach the castle on that momentous day.

As more and more people became alert, there was a rising clamor, as they questioned each other and looked around for missing companions. Sir Edgar stood on the dais, raising his hands for quiet, and, when that didn't work, letting out a sharp whistle. The voices subsided into a murmur.

"I know that many of you have heard the gossip regarding the princess," Sir Edgar said, and some of the courtiers looked around guiltily. "Their Majesties tried their best to keep the situation quiet, but under the circumstances, I feel I can confirm to you that the rumors are absolutely true."

The noise level began to rise again.

"At Princess Aurora's christening, Indigo did indeed condemn the princess to death on her sixteenth birthday. The fairy Lilac managed to save her, by changing the sentence to a hundred-year sleep. The princess is now in this sleep, and, somehow, we seem to be in it with her. And whoever or whatever brought us here apparently saw fit to leave the king and queen and the others who were in the castle behind."

The room exploded in shouts and exclamations. Aurora stood in her usual spot at the back of the dais taking in the scene and feeling progressively worse and worse; it was her fault, all of it. Slowly, she took a step forward and then another. Eventually, she stood even with Sir Edgar, though she had no idea what to do next.

One by one, the occupants of the great hall noticed her standing there and began to fall silent. With all those eyes on her, Aurora was nearly frozen in fear, but she clasped her hands in front of her and began to speak.

"I'm sorry," she said, a slight quaver in her voice. "I never intended for any of this to happen. None of you should be here. I wish I could end this or send you back, but I can't ... I don't know how."

And a tear slid down her cheek.

No one in the hall moved or made a sound. Aurora started to think they might stay like that forever, until she heard a commotion near the wall to her right. A child in shabby, tattered clothes, perhaps a helper from the stables or even a villager who had snuck into the castle hoping for some food, emerged from the crowd and walked up to the dais. He held out his hand, offering a grubby handkerchief to Aurora.

Aurora felt a pang in her chest at this simple act of humble kindness, something altogether too rare in her world. She knelt and took the handkerchief, ignoring its less than pristine state. She smiled down at the boy, who beamed back up at her.

"Thank you, good sir," she said, and she felt a shift in the room, as some of the tension dissipated and more smiles appeared here and there.

Aurora stood, wiping the tears from her cheeks (though she used her hand, not the handkerchief). She felt calmer now, less frantic, as she turned to Sir Edgar.

"We don't know how long we are going to be here," she said. "But we should probably figure out how to make everyone comfortable, yes?"

Sir Edgar watched her, his eyes unreadable, and then gave a sharp nod.

"Yes," he said. "Let's do that."

A quick reconnaissance of the dream castle revealed that all the rooms in the real version were present and accounted for, so everyone had a place to stay;

in the end, though, most ended up spending the majority of their time in the great hall, finding comfort in the camaraderie. Patrols were assembled to explore the grounds and the surrounding wood, to see what lay beyond, but no matter how long they walked or which direction they took, they always ended up back at the castle.

"Unnatural," Sir Edgar muttered, gazing out a window at the wood.

"No," Lord Dorian said, stepping up beside him. "Only magical. It's true to the nature of the dream."

It was a strange nature, to be sure. None of the children grew, and none of the adults seemed to age at all. They never perspired or shivered or ached. They became phantoms, drifting through the castle and yearning for the freedom that was maddeningly beyond their reach.

There was no day or night in the dreaming, only a long stretch of in-between time. When the courtiers wanted food, they ate, more for the novelty of flavor than for sustenance. When they were tired, they rested (they never really slept, for they were already asleep). And, when they were bored, which was often, they found ways to amuse themselves.

The ladies of the court gave dancing lessons. There were endless games of Prisoner's Base and Nine Men's Morris. Sometimes, they would move the tables aside to play Nine Pins. At one point, after a meal, when everyone was sitting around the fire telling stories, Sir Edgar noticed Aurora eying his sword. Quietly, he drew it from its scabbard and held it out to her.

"Oh, no," she said. "I couldn't."

"Go ahead," he said. "Take it."

Tentatively, Aurora reached out and put her hand around the grip. As soon as Sir Edgar let go, the point dropped to the floor with a clang.

"It's heavy!" Aurora exclaimed.

"You get used to it," Sir Edgar said, amused. "Try again."

With an effort, Aurora lifted the sword and held it in front of her with both hands. Her eyes were bright as she watched the firelight flicker on the metal.

"Would you like me to teach you?" Sir Edgar asked.

"The sword?" she said.

"Yes."

"Really?"

"Yes."

Aurora's face broke into a delighted smile.

"I would like that very much."

She gave the sword an experimental swing, which immediately turned into a wild arc as the weight threw her off balance.

Sir Edgar reached out and grabbed Aurora's arm, taking the sword and sliding it back into the scabbard.

"Perhaps we should start with staffs."

When she wasn't working with Sir Edgar, Aurora found herself spending time with Lord Dorian. He was a wise and learned man, who knew about all kinds of things—medicine and the law and the history of Aurora's kingdom. And he did know quite a bit about magic, which he always discussed with the type of humble modesty that was really showing off.

But his great passion was chess, and he set about teaching it to Aurora.

As they sat at one of the tables in the great hall, Lord Dorian moved his bishop.

"Checkmate," he said.

Aurora's mouth fell open, and she examined the board. When she spotted the way he had her cornered, she let out a frustrated groan and dropped her head to the table.

"'You're getting better," Lord Dorian said as he

started resetting the board.

Aurora lifted her head but remained slumped, clearly dejected.

"You still always beat me, though."

"You don't vary your attack enough," he said. "You rely too much on your queen."

"But the queen is the most powerful piece," she said.

"She is," he said, looking over the tops of his spectacles. "But she is still part of an army. She can accomplish far more with the other pieces' support than she can on her own."

Aurora crossed her arms, scowling, but said nothing.

"Patience, my dear," he said as he rose to get a glass of wine. "You'll get it."

"I'm tired of being patient," she grumbled. "I want to get out."

But their confinement dragged on, and so Aurora poured her frustration into her training. As it turned out, she had a fair degree of natural proficiency in combat, but that in and of itself was not enough for Sir Edgar. He was constantly challenging her, pushing her to develop her skills. They were in the thick of one of their bouts when he broke past her defenses and delivered a solid blow to her knuckles. She dropped her staff, cradling her smarting hand and fighting back curses she had overheard in the stables.

Sir Edgar lowered his staff as well.

"Are you all right, Your Highness?"

"Yes," she said, annoyed at him and at herself. "It was a stupid mistake. And I do wish you wouldn't call me that. I think we're well past formalities."

Sir Edgar cocked his head, gazing at her, then shrugged.

"Very well … Aurora."

This time it was Aurora's turn to stop and gaze.

"What is it?" he said.

"I just … thought you might argue more," she said sheepishly.

Sir Edgar bent over and picked up her staff, holding it out to her.

"In the army," he said, "one must work hard to procure their rank. It seems a sensible system to me."

"Ah," Aurora said, chastened a bit. "I see."

Sir Edgar raised his staff.

"Ready for another go?"

Aurora raised hers as well.

"Ready."

They continued, but before long, Sir Edgar parried one of her blows, and, as she tried to recover, she tripped, falling against the wall. She growled in annoyance.

"It's these skirts," he said, poking gently at her hem with the tip of his staff. "They limit your movement."

"Well, what else am I supposed to wear?" she snapped.

He looked thoughtful for a moment, then called out, "Lady Adeline!"

Aurora's former nursemaid bustled over from where she had been listening to the children practice reading. As they explained the situation, Lady Adeline pursed her lips and muttered things under her breath that sounded like "not at all proper" and "beneath her station," but she nevertheless sent the children scampering through the castle, looking for anything that might meet the princess's needs.

Before long, there was a small pile of clothing on the floor near the fire, salvaged from a host of abandoned chests and wardrobes, and without too much trial and error, they found a tunic and pair of leggings that fit Aurora tolerably well, as well as a sturdy pair of boots and a belt. She had long since taken the pins from her hair and begun wearing it in a single plait, which now hung over her shoulder.

"What do you think?" she said, holding out her arms and turning slowly in front of Sir Edgar and Lady Adeline.

"I think you look very fine," Sir Edgar said approvingly. "Very fine indeed. What say you, my lady?"

Next to him, Lady Adeline examined Aurora with her fingers pressed to her mouth.

"I suppose it will do," she said. "If it is absolutely necessary."

But there was a hint of pride in her voice, and her eyes were warm.

The new clothes gave Aurora much greater freedom of movement, and before long, Sir Edgar decided it was time to move from staffs to swords. He found one for Aurora's use in the armory (well-balanced, if still far inferior to his), and she took to it with relish.

During one of their sparring sessions, Lord Dorian lounged nearby, watching and drinking a cup of wine. Lady Adeline sat next to him, working on some knitting.

"You're doing very well," Sir Edgar said when they finished.

"Fine lot of good it will do as long as we're stuck here," Aurora grumbled.

"I've been giving that some thought," said Lord Dorian. "I'm a bit of a student of magic, you know."

"Are you?" said Lady Adeline archly. "You hadn't mentioned."

"And I wondered," said Lord Dorian, ignoring her. "Why don't we just try asking for a way out?"

They all looked at him, bewildered.

"Asking who?" said Aurora.

"Well, Lilac, of course."

Sir Edgar snorted.

"And how do you propose she does that?"

Lord Dorian turned to Aurora.

"Didn't you say Indigo told you the dreaming let you see her? Let you talk to her?"

"Yes," Aurora said hesitantly.

"Well, make a request," he said. "Tell the dreaming you want to talk to Lilac. See what happens."

It seemed a far-fetched idea, but nobody had any better ones, so later, Aurora stepped out onto the path in front of the castle. She closed her eyes and took a deep breath.

I'd like to see the fairy Lilac, she thought. *Please.*

At first, nothing happened, but then, the light began to fade until all Aurora could see was blackness.

Then she felt a sense of movement, a breeze on her face, and slowly, the light returned.

Aurora was now standing before a beautiful house surrounded by lush greenery, with a small waterfall in the distance. It was a simple house, but large, and constructed of fine wood and stone. Cautiously, she climbed the steps outside and went in the front door.

At the end of a long hall, she found a doorway leading to an airy library. Stepping over the threshold, she saw Lilac sitting at a large table, writing in a leather-bound book. When she heard Aurora's footsteps, Lilac lifted her head, and after a startled moment, smiled.

"Aurora," she said. "How lovely to see you."

"And you, my lady," Aurora said, and, unsure of what else to do, bobbed a curtsy, something she had only done a handful of times in her life.

Lilac closed her book and pushed back from the table.

"It feels an age since we last met," she said, walking across the room towards Aurora and then around her, looking her up and down. "Don't you look … jaunty."

"Thank you, my lady," said Aurora, feeling increasingly wrong-footed.

"Come, sit down," Lilac said, gesturing to a sitting

area where a tray waited, laden with wine, glasses, and a bowl of fruit. Aurora was fairly certain the tray had not been there the moment before.

Hesitantly, she took a seat and waited for Lilac to pour each of them a cup of wine. This was not going as she had expected. She had thought Lilac would know what she needed, why she was there. But the fairy seemed to have no idea at all.

"Now," she said, handing Aurora a goblet and settling back into her own seat. "What can I do for you?"

For a moment, Aurora grappled to find any words, but eventually, she took a deep breath and spoke.

"I have questions" she said. "About the spell."

Lilac's face darkened ever so slightly.

"Oh?"

"Yes," Aurora hurried on. "My parents explained it to me, of course, when I was young. They also told me to stay away from spinning wheels, but …"

Lilac nodded. "The call was too strong," she said, knowingly. "Indigo is old and her magic is formidable."

"Yes," said Aurora. "And once it happened, once I'd pricked my finger, I recognized the sleep. I knew where I was and why, but … It's so strange here in the dreaming, and there are people here with me and I don't understand. I don't understand at all."

Lilac's face was inscrutable for a moment, but then she took Aurora's hand in both of hers.

"Of course, you don't," she said, her voice soothing. "And I'm afraid that's my fault. I should have talked to you about it a long time ago. But I will tell you now.

"We fairies can see into the true hearts of things, you know. And as soon as you were born, we could see you had such potential. In you, we saw the beginnings of someone wise and just and kind, all wonderful qualities in a queen.

"But your heart was wild—full of passion and fire. We could see you becoming too loud, too hasty, too much. There was a chance you would prove ... disruptive."

"Disruptive," Aurora repeated, her insides turning cold.

"There is an order to the world, my dear, but maintaining it is a tricky business," Lilac went on, seemingly unaware of Aurora's distress. "The council of fairy elders has managed the balance of power between the kingdoms for centuries, and we have done so by choosing our leaders carefully and planning for every eventuality. We wanted you to succeed, but you needed taming. Only we didn't know how best to accomplish that; it was a matter of some debate.

"Indigo tried to go around us, the fool," she said disdainfully. "She said such a constricted life was worse than death; she always was dramatic. So she cast her spell, and our plans seemed for naught, but I quickly realized there was an opportunity. There was a small chance you could defy the magic and resist pricking your finger, in which case we would set about training you, reining you in. But if you didn't, you could sleep, a good long sleep that would allow you to ... mellow."

Aurora's mind raced. She remembered being a little girl and Lady Adeline being sent away. The ladies that came to care for her then had been stern and cold, always scolding her.

Sit still, Aurora. Calm down, Aurora. Be quiet, Aurora.

And she had. Under their constant pressure, she had become a meek, untethered thing. Hidden from the world, isolated and lonely. And it was all in service of Lilac's notions of maintaining order. Of control.

"I knew that it might take a long while, but you would mature into a queen we could be proud of. As for the others, we knew it would be hard for you to wake separated from everyone and everything you knew, so I spelled them as well, so you would have help adjusting to your new life. And I enchanted the wood so no one would disturb you."

At this, the fog of pain and sadness in Aurora's head began to clear, sharpening her focus.

"But those people have families," she stammered. "Homes, loved ones."

Lilac sighed.

"That is unfortunate, I must say," she said. "But you have to understand. It's for the greater good."

Aurora's fingers tightened around her cup.

"I can't let you do this," she said quietly. "I won't."

Lilac's lip twitched into a hint of a sneer.

"I don't see that you have much of a choice, my dear," she said. "You're bound in magic for the foreseeable future."

"But it's not right," said Aurora. "It's not fair."

"Of course it's not fair!" Lilac snapped. "When it comes to making the big decisions, nothing is fair. There is only what must be done by those strong enough to do it."

"You said you knew me to be just," said Aurora. "How can you know that and think I will accept this? The sleep, the 'order', any of it?"

Lilac only stared at her, eyes burning.

Slowly, Aurora stood, setting her glass carefully on the table.

"I will discover a way to break the magic," she said calmly. "And once I am awake, I will find you again."

Lilac's face twisted in anger as Aurora made her way across the room.

"You're just a spoiled child," she spat. "How exactly do you think this is going to end? If you challenge me, who do you think will win?"

Aurora pushed the door open and spoke without turning back.

"We shall see."

When she arrived back at the castle, Aurora immediately gathered Sir Edgar, Lord Dorian, and Lady Adeline and told them what Lilac had said. When she finished, they all stared at each other in shock.

"They've been manipulating us," Sir Edgar said gravely. "All this time."

"I always wondered why they took me away from you," Lady Adeline said, her voice shaking with anger. "Now I know."

"There must be some way to break the magic," Aurora said urgently. "Do you have any ideas, Lord

Dorian? Any at all?"

"Perhaps," said Lord Dorian, and he pursed his lips, gazing into the fire.

"Well," Lady Adeline said impatiently. "Out with it."

"I believe," Lord Dorian said slowly, "That Aurora may be able to go back the way she came."

"Do you mean by pricking my finger again?" Aurora said.

"Yes," said Lord Dorian.

They all looked at him skeptically, and he sighed.

"I did say perhaps."

Aurora sat back in her chair, thinking.

"If that does somehow work," she said slowly. "Will the rest of you wake up, too?"

"I'm not sure," Lord Dorian said. "From what you've said, it sounds like Lilac used a separate spell on us, so it's very likely that even if you wake, the rest of us will sleep on."

"Plus, there is the enchantment around the wood to contend with," mused Sir Edgar.

Aurora kicked at a footstool irritably.

"I will find a way to get you out of this," she said.

Lady Adeline took her hand.

"Of course you will," she said, and her voice wasn't

consoling or patronizing, only confident.

"Has anyone seen a spinning wheel here?" Aurora asked.

Everyone shook their heads.

"If the dreaming let you talk to Lilac," said Lord Dorian. "It might be on our side; it might want you to get out. Perhaps it will provide."

It was possible he was right, but that didn't do much for Aurora's mood. Feeling peevish and restless, she stepped out into the perpetual twilight to take a walk. She didn't venture far this time—just a few laps around the castle—but it helped to work off some of her nervous energy.

When she went back inside, she started to return to the great hall, but as she was about to turn the final corner, she stopped. A familiar feeling came over her like a cold gust of air—a pull towards her old bedroom, much like the one she had felt on her birthday that had led to her pricking her finger in the first place. But it did not have the same power over her this time. Slowly, she walked through the cold, stone hallways towards her room, not because she had to, but because she wanted to.

When she reached her door, she gently pushed it

open. And there, on the floor next to her bed, shining faintly, was a spinning wheel.

Aurora let one small, relieved laugh and steadied herself on the doorframe.

"Thank you," she whispered.

Later, Aurora stood at the back of the great hall, listening to the excited buzz as the courtiers rushed around sharing the news. At first, she had wanted to keep her discovery secret, for fear of getting everybody's hopes up only to have them dashed. But her advisers—for that is what Sir Edgar, Lord Dorian, and Lady Adeline had become—had convinced her to share it, so she had. Now, the time was nearing for her to go, and all of them were counting on her.

Lady Adeline approached with a crowd of children around her, bubbling with excitement.

"Go on," she said as they reached Aurora, and she gave one of the girls a nudge.

The girl, small and shy, stepped forward and held out a large handful of wildflowers to Aurora.

"There's one here from each of us," she blurted, clearly nervous.

"They're wishes," one of the boys supplied helpfully. "For you to beat the bad fairy."

Aurora took the flowers and bent down to kiss each of the children who had spoken on the cheek.

"Thank you," she said to all the children, tucking the flowers into her tunic. "I promise I'll do my best."

Lord Dorian approached then, as Lady Adeline ushered the children away, and pressed a white pawn from the chessboard into Aurora's hand.

"What is this for?" she asked.

"Luck," he said. "Courage. Whatever you need."

"Will it go with me once I … once I'm awake?"

"I believe so," he said. "But even if it doesn't …" He reached up and touched Aurora's temple. "What you need is here."

Aurora nodded.

"And don't forget, my dear—the queen is powerful, but she is not alone."

"I'll remember," she said, and he squeezed her shoulder before he stepped away.

She turned towards the door then, but before she got far, Sir Edgar was in her path. He stood still and quiet for a moment, then held out his sword to her. She took a step back.

"I can't take that," she told him.

"I insist, Your Highness" he said.

"I told you not to call me that."

"I will, because it is who you are" he said. "Because you have earned it."

She looked away, eyes shining with tears, and he hefted the sword again.

"I wish I could go with you, but I can at least send you with this. And you can bring us home."

She swallowed around the lump in her throat and nodded, wrapping her free hand around the hilt of the sword. And she walked out of the great hall for the last time.

Her hands trembled as she walked into her bedroom, but her back was straight and her chin high. When she reached the spinning wheel, she took a deep breath and raised the hand still clutching the pawn, a single finger extended to touch the spindle. Then darkness descended, and she felt herself falling, down, down, down...

In the castle behind the enchanted wood, Princess Aurora woke ninety-nine years early, with a sword in one hand, a chess piece in the other, and a bouquet of wishes next to her heart.

And in the waking world, she walked.

Alison Ching loved books so much growing up that she decided to make them her job. She taught high school English for three years before getting a master's degree in library science from the University of North Texas; at this point, she has worked as a school librarian at the elementary, middle, and high school levels. Her writing has appeared in professional library publications and the anthology *Supernatural Youth: The Rise of the Teen Hero in Literature and Popular Culture*. She is a proud Hufflepuff.

Redemption

Madeline Smoot

As a child, he never did revel in the glories of war. He never understood the appeal of drab uniforms or why someone would want to leave home for battlefields and bullets. So, when war was declared he didn't join his school mates who flocked to the recruitment office. He didn't lie about his age for the privilege of being shot at by enemy soldiers or, worse, having to aim his rifle and shoot at one of them. He didn't regret his decision.

He did, though, get tired of finding goose and chicken feathers piled on his school books, tied to the pail he used to milk the cow, and handed to him by pretty girls he had once admired. He soon learned to ignore his weeping mother and her ceaseless wailing about her "shameful" and "disgraceful" son. When his friends began returning from the war in pine boxes, he avoided the funerals where the bereaved glared at him and all but said they wished it was him being lowered into the ground instead of some beautiful, brave boy who had gone to defend his country.

He could have borne all this—the feathers, the weeping, even the condemnation—with nothing more than a sigh and a shake of his head as he went about his studies and his chores on the farm. It was his father's mournful eyes, his disappointed air that he could have raised such a coward for a son, that finally drove that son to the recruitment office.

One week later much to his father's pride and his mother's open relief, he boarded the train headed to the capital with the other able-bodied (and often younger) boys who would soon march for the glory of Empire. In the capital they gave him the drab uniform that made girls swoon. With a grim smile, he tried to pretend that girls swooning and sneaking him kisses made up for the rest of it. It didn't.

They loaded him down with supplies like canteens and cigarettes. They distributed a rucksack filled with a blanket, edible if unappetizing rations, and ammunition. In a more ominous twist, they strapped a gas mask to his belt. They handed him a riffle which he knew how to use and a handgun which he did not. Then because the war was going badly for the Brotherland, they dispensed with training and loaded him on a train for the Southern

Front.

He bore the No Man's Land of war for one year. A year of terror and boredom huddled in trenches, staring out at a hellscape unimagined by the poets of the past. He survived machine gun fire and shelling and bombs filled with gas dropped from high flying aerial balloons. Each day he stared straight ahead and aimed his riffle and guarded his eyes from the debris that flew from the dirt walls when a bullet struck them.

On his 428th day of the war, he was rotated out of the trenches for some leave in a neighboring town. The town had been decimated by long range shells, and the rotting husks of the buildings weren't much better than the trenches he had just escaped. After a night spent in a molding canvas tent filled with the cigarette smoke of his mates, he decided to walk in the woods that bordered the town. He needed fresh air he told the sentry at the gate. The man nodded and reminded him to be back before sunset or he would be locked out and perhaps presumed a deserter.

He walked through the trees, surprised by the silence and the distance the forest seemed to place between him and the war. The leaves rustled in the wind and didn't sound at all like bullets shrieking through the air. He jumped when a squirrel dropped onto the forest floor near him, and then gave a short laugh filled with everything except humor when he realized the thump hadn't been the warning to duck away from a grenade.

He reached the point where he needed to turn back if he was to return to the village by sunset. He kept walking. He kept walking for days.

At some point he raided a farmer's clothes line. This far from the front, the only people in uniform were messengers and deserters. Back in the trenches he had heard tales of men that had gone mad. They'd run from the frontline screaming and foaming at the mouth. The good citizens of the countryside were said to be terrified of deserters and the havoc they brought. He didn't think he fit that description exactly, but he didn't feel like being shot on sight. He threw his uniform in the farmer's refuse heap. He buried the little metal disks he had worn around his neck, the ones that had been meant for identification should he have found himself too close to an exploding grenade.

He walked through the wood with no real destination in mind other than away. Away from the war and his friends, dead from a bullet or sick from the gas. Away from his family and village where he had proven their worst fears of his cowardice. Away from the Brotherland where only a noose awaited a boy that left his duty without leave.

He stuck to the woods and the forest and followed streams uphill towards their sources. During the summer and fall there was no shortage of food he could forage, and he created a makeshift pack to carry excess supplies. He continued to hike through the woods that now carpeted the edges of mountains. He continued on his quest for up and away.

When winter began to set in, he started to worry for the first time. In the evenings his shivering could no longer be ignored. His two wool shirts were not enough to protect him from the morning frosts, and he wondered what he would do when the first snows came. The plants with the berries had died off, and the trees with the fruit had lost their leaves and begun their long season of hibernation. There were still a few nuts on the ground, overlooked by the more enterprising animals, but he couldn't depend on the random nut or two to get him through the winter.

Worried as he sorted through the remaining supplies in his pack, he lost his footing and tumbled to the ground.

A low cackling laugh seemed to appreciate his fall. He rolled until he could sit up and found himself on some sort of forest track. This one seemed a bit more intentional than the wandering game paths he had followed through the forest during his journey. At the base of what might have once been a well sat a hunched old woman half-way hidden by her thick cloak and nearly doubled over in her enjoyment at his expense.

He frowned. His ego had been slightly bruised by the fall, but that would only take moments to mend. A woman as old and infirm as the one next to the rocks would not have been able to hobble far from her home, even with the walking stick she clutched in one of her shaking hands. That meant he must be closer to some village than he had anticipated. Although he had no idea where exactly he was after his months of ambling through the woods and the foothills of the mountains, he did assume he was still either in the Brotherland or one of its allies. Avoiding villages seemed like the safest recourse.

"Good morning, Grandmother," the soldier said in a polite tone while he pulled himself up to his feet. He might be a coward and a deserter, but he could still be unfailingly polite. He gave her a small bow as well.

"And to you, child," she said back. Her cackles subsided down into small chuckles. "That was quite the fall."

"A mere misstep."

"Hmm." The old woman stared at him through the milky film of old age that covered her eyes. "If you say so."

He shifted his weight from one foot to the other, uncomfortable from her stare and unsure if they still spoke of his stumble.

"May I be of service, Grandmother?" he asked in an effort to turn the conversation. "Are you in need of help to your home?" He didn't want to enter a village. Even without the telltale uniform, the soldier felt that with just a glance any person he met (at least someone not half blind) would be able to see his cowardice as if a yellow C had been emblazoned on his forehead. If he was lucky, villagers would merely run him out of town. Most likely they would capture him and return him to the capital to the army and the noose.

"Brave one, aren't you?" the woman asked as if she had read his thoughts and was now mocking them.

His muscles stiffened as if he'd been hit by the rigidity that strikes the body some hours after death. "I would not call myself that."

"I don't suppose you would." The old woman sighed

and shifted as if to make her spot on the ground more comfortable. "No, child, I do not need help home. My home is just over there." She pointed with her stick at a thicket so dense, he couldn't see what lay behind. He supposed she might have a hut of some sort hidden within the brambles.

She stared at him again in that disconcerting way although he could not fathom how she could make out much with such cloudy eyes. "I do require aid," she said just when he had decided to make his excuses and be on his way.

"How may I assist?" he asked. He wanted to tell her to get on with it, but that would be rude. He might be a gutless milksop, but he wasn't rude.

"I find myself short of food for my mid-day meal. Do you have any sustenance to share?"

Both of them turned to the small pack held in his hand.

For a second his self-preservation had him almost clutching his pack to his chest. The soldier had very little food as it was, and he was already worried over his dwindling supplies. Then he relaxed a bit and nearly shook his head at his foolishness. Even with careful hoarding, his food would only last a day at the most. It wasn't enough for him to live on, but it would make a decent meal for the old woman. Besides, he was young and strong, even if he wasn't as strong as he'd been before his days in the trenches. He could find more food if needed. The old woman most likely could not. Perhaps when he saw her settled back home she would be able to point him to a town where he might find people who needed workers and who didn't ask questions.

"It's not much." He knelt beside her and placed the pack in her lap. "There's an older apple and some nuts and some berries dried by the sun."

"It is a feast fit for a queen," the old woman said in a soft voice. She gave him a gentle pat on the arm.

He tried to smile, but his worry kept the smile from forming into anything more than a half-hearted grin.

"What would you ask in return for this generosity?"

"Directions if you would be so kind." The soldier stood back up and stared down the forest track for a moment before turning back. "Do you know of a place where I might earn my keep? A place where my absence from the battlefields will not be noted?" He added the last bit in an undertone, positive a woman of her age would not hear.

She cocked her head at him with a bemused expression. "In return for giving me your last bit of food, you only seek directions?"

He nodded, unsure why that mattered.

She sighed again and shook her head. "And you think yourself a coward. Very well," she added before he could respond in outrage for having labeled him so plainly. She sat up a bit straighter and seemed to be considering. "A place to earn your keep." She stared into the distance, thinking. It must have been a trick of the light, but he could have sworn the film in her eyes faded away until they seemed as clear as his. A smile filled her face, erasing the wrinkles he'd sworn had crisscrossed her skin like a railroad map of the Brotherland.

"I have just the thing." Her eyes sparkled in the sunlight, and he could not fathom how he had ever thought them the eyes of an old woman. "Not far from here, a man sits in his home worried over his dozen daughters. Each night he locks them in their suite with an army of guards, and each morning he finds them exhausted with the soles of their slippers worn through. No one knows what the ladies do each night, and none have been able to bring it to a halt. Some say they pace from their confinement, others that they dance the night away in a magical world of pleasure."

He snorted at that. "It sounds like a fairy tale." In this scientific age of bombs and gases, everyone knew magic was not real and fairy tales did not exist. A world that was filled with trenches and places like the Southern Front had no room in it for happily ever afters. "You speak of the Helvetian king and his daughters. There have been rumors about them for years." Even before the war he had heard the tales of the isolated king and his eccentric daughters. "They are just rumors."

The woman shook her head and the hood of her cloak slid all the way down. From the wisps that had escaped before, he had assumed her hair was as snow white as his own grandmother's locks, but this woman had yellow hair so light it was almost white.

"They are very real, and the distress to their father is acute. The princesses themselves would not mind an end to their nightly ordeals." She cocked her head to the side considering him. He shifted slightly to avoid such a penetrating stare. "Yes." Her head nodded up and down in a slow, almost hypnotic, motion. "I think you are just the one to save them."

A laugh escaped from his throat, filled with all the anger and fear and self-loathing that had been festering in his heart since his first night in the woods. "If what you say is true, these princesses need a hero. I'm no hero. I'm not the one to save anyone."

The woman (how could he have ever though her old?) began to smile. Her teeth were sharper than a normal woman's, but even so her smile wasn't malicious. Disconcerting, but not terrifying. She spoke in a casual tone that belied the seriousness of her words. "Perhaps, then, they will save you."

By the time he reached the outskirts of Adventia, the capital of Helvetii, the soldier firmly believed in magic. Like in a fairy tale, the woman (although he now doubted she was something as pedestrian as a mortal woman) had gifted him three items before setting him on his path.

She had returned his pack, only his slim stores were gone, replaced by food truly fit for a Queen's table. What's more, it never ran out. For the first time since his train ride to the Southern Front, he had three full meals a day, and his form began to once again fill out.

She then handed him the cloak off her back, and he

had discovered that the garment did more than keep a boy warm. It also seemed to turn his fellow travelers' gazes away from him as if he had become invisible. This allowed him to avoid unwanted questions and hitch a ride on a number of unsuspecting farmers' carts.

Finally, she gave him a small metal mug not unlike the cups they used on the frontline for their rations. "Do not drink from any other vessel," she had warned. The soldier had taken her at her word, and he discovered that the cup turned even the vilest looking liquid into pure spring water. Just to be certain, he had siphoned off a small amount of fuel from an abandoned motorcycle near the Helvetti border. What should have been pure poison did not even give him a cramp.

Countless times on the road he had considered turning around, of disappearing back into the woods. With the witch's gift he needn't fear the coming of winter. Afraid to anger such a powerful being though, he had followed her directions to the capital, committed to his task to save the princesses.

The morning he arrived in Adventia, he traded some of the fine food in his pack for some fresher, better quality clothes. Although Helvetti had not joined the war like nearly every other country in the world, they were still affected by the food shortages now plaguing much of the continent. Shopkeepers that would have once turned their nose up at such barter were happy to outfit him in a suit and new shoes for pastries and fresh vegetables and steak and kidney pies. No one asked where he had acquired such rare items. He did not volunteer the information.

When the bells of the cathedral tolled out the midday hour, he joined the queue of citizens waiting for an audience with the king. Helvetti was a monarchy in the old classical sense with no parliament or congress constraining the king's hand. The courts might hear the ordinary arguments of the day, but anyone from the highest Duchess to the lowest newsboy could air their grievances with the king, provided they were willing to wait.

He waited four days. During that time, he willingly shared his food from his pack. He didn't share so much that people became suspicious, but he shared enough to become popular with his fellow supplicants. When it was finally his turn before the throne, he announced in a loud, clear tone the words the witch had given him. "I am here to solve the mystery of the princesses."

The hall went silent. The secretaries froze with

their hands over the keys of their typewriters, and the hushed whispering cut off as if someone had flicked a switch on a wireless set.

"Are ye daft?" an old man muttered from behind him. Like a dam breaking during a flood, the room exploded with the roiling noise of conversation.

On one of the thrones before him, the Crown Princess narrowed her eyes at him. "Not another one," she muttered to one of her younger sisters at her left. He couldn't hear her over the roar of the crowd's disbelief, but he could read her lips. The Crown Princess and heir to Helvetti's throne was a good deal older than him, nearly thirty, but her sister looked closer to him in age. She smiled at him, but the smile held no warmth or joy. If she had burst into tears, she couldn't have conveyed more sadness than that one little smile.

"He looks nice," her lips said.

The king held up his hand and silence slowly fell over the room once more.

"It has been nearly a year since one has tried to discover the cause of my daughters' exhaustion and why their new shoes are ruined in an evening. Nearly a year since I last executed the man who failed."

The younger princess winced and looked away.

"How are they executed?" he asked the king, irritated that the witch had neglected this little detail. He had been safe enough from the hangman's noose in Helvetti. Not only did they not care about the war raging beyond their borders, they didn't have much interest in the deserters and other refugees trickling into their high mountain nation. The fact that the country was difficult to access with few mountain passes that would be clear come winter meant that the numbers trickling in were not large enough to worry the existing population.

"I have them executed by firing squad. Are you sure you still wish to solve the mystery?"

At least it wasn't a noose. The soldier stared at the Crown Princess with the pursed lips and the younger princess who shook her head with a violence that caused her diadem to nearly fly off her head.

"If you do solve it," continued the king, not actually waiting for an answer, "you will be elevated to the rank of duke and be given holdings in the Everfast region. You will also marry my oldest daughter, Louisa, and become her consort upon her ascension to the throne."

Louisa's lips pursed even further like she'd just sucked on a lemon of unsurpassed sourness. She looked how he felt at the prospect. The witch had neglected

Redemption 207

to mention this part as well. He had thought he would solve the mystery, be given some gold, and be on his way. He had come to please an old witch who had given him magical gifts not to earn a Duchy.

"Again, do you still wish to risk death to solve the mystery?"

When the king put it that way, the soldier rather thought he did not. For a second he considered turning and walking away from the castle and Helvetii. It was what his parents and the village back home would expect of him after all. He had walked away from the army and the frontline. He could leave, but then, what? Would the witch appear and reclaim her gifts? Would she denounce him for the coward that he was, ensuring no one else would offer him a job ever again?

He stood before the thrones and the princess with the sad eyes, the one with the irritated expression, and the king who had begun to look a bit mad.

He had promised the witch he would save the princesses, and he would keep his word. He might be a lily-livered skulker, but he wasn't an oath-breaker.

Besides, he had a cloak that rendered him invisible. If he did not find the source of the princesses' ruined shoes, he could always sneak away before daybreak.

"I wish to stay," he said in a quiet voice that seemed to ring out in the quieter room. The younger princess sighed and looked away.

"You have one night," said the king.

The soldier spent the day meeting the twelve princesses from the heir, Princess Louisa, who at twenty-eight had very little time for a boy of nineteen, all the way down to the youngest, the Princess Elise, a mere ten years old. Princess Elise reminded him of his own dear sister before she succumbed to the 'flu that swept through their village seven long years before.

Most of the day though was spent in the company of the other princess who had attended court that morning, the seventh princess, Princess Mary. Only a year younger than him, he found that he had more in common with her than her sisters. Before he left school to spend a disastrous year on the Southern Front, he had been curious about all things chemical and the almost magical reactions unrelated substances could produce. A year wearing gas masks and ducking the deadly inventions created by the chemistry he had once admired had cured him of this fascination.

Although she had never been to school, Princess

Mary and her sisters had shared some of the finest tutors the king could bring to his court. Her knowledge far surpassed his, and her enthusiasm and sincere admiration of the subject began to rekindle in him an interest he had long thought dead.

Too soon, though, the dining table in the Princesses' apartment was laid with supper, and the soldier sat down with the twelve girls for a fine, if simple, meal. Although the fare was limited, the wine was not. After Princess Louisa pressed a third glass on him, he began to suspect the princess of trying to get him drunk. If the other fools had succumbed to the pretty girls' smiles and the intoxicating effects of wine, then it was no wonder none had discovered their secrets.

He appeared to drink their wine in large amounts with good grace. He even pretended to become drunk and slur his words. However, since he insisted on using his own small metal cup given to him by the witch, he drank nothing but clear spring water the entire meal.

At the end of the meal, he pretended to be drowsy and to drop off in his chair there at the table.

"Finally," said Princess Louisa. Her chair shoved back with a screech as she stood. "Another fool for the firing squad."

"He wasn't a fool," said Princess Mary. A cool hand rested against his cheek for a moment. "He was sweet and funny and an intelligent man."

"He's a dead man now." Louisa's caustic tone drew at least one sharp gasp.

"Louisa!" hissed one of the other sisters.

"What?" asked Louisa. From the clattering around him, the girls had begun gathering up the remains of the dinner. "I speak the truth, and you all know it. I am sorry that Mary likes the boy. I'm sorry I had to drug him into insensibility, but what can we do? Have him carrying tales to Father about the portal and the demons on the other side? I value his life and regret it will be lost, but I value our souls more."

On that ominous note, she stormed to the door that separated the princesses' living space from the rest of the palace. She banged on it until servants appeared. From the noise she made, she all but shoved the dishes onto their waiting trays. When everything had been cleared to Louisa's satisfaction, the door was shut again. In silence the princesses waited while multiple locks clicked into place and a final thump meant the large wooden bar had been lowered sealing them in.

"That's that," said Mary.

"Come, sisters. We must prepare for the night," said Louisa.

The women filed out past the table until the room sat empty. Cautiously, the soldier waited to be sure none would come back before opening his eyes. Placing his enchanted cup back in his pack, he drew on his cloak and pulled up the hood. He then went in search of the princesses. He found them gathering in a lovely room that must normally be used for socializing, art, and other amusements common among high born ladies. As expected, they had changed into new shoes. He had not expected to see them dressed as if ready for battle. Instead of the gowns they had worn earlier, all of them, even little Elise, now wore clothes reminiscent of a cavalry officer. Each had a crisp white blouse tucked into breeches. Each had at least one sword strapped to her side and more than a few had daggers in convenient sheaths strapped to legs and upper arms. The twins each carried matching bows and three quivers filled with arrows. Louisa was armed to the neck with two bandoliers of bullets and revolvers strapped to the outside of each thigh. She also carried two sabres and appeared to be warming up by thrusting them at a nearby pillow. Feathers fluttered to the floor after each strike.

He recognized the nervous energy filling the room. He had experienced it twice before on the front. He had participated in two campaigns to push the enemy army back. Both campaigns had resulted in gains that could only be measured in inches. The night before both, the trenches had filled with men wondering if that night was their last.

He still didn't know what Louisa had meant by portals and demons, but one thing was clear. The princesses weren't ruining their footwear by dancing all night.

A delicate clock on the mantle chimed the eleventh hour, and the girls stopped their feverish preparations. A sigh escaped from one of the girl's lips, but he couldn't tell which one. He knew this feeling too. He too had filled with the calm of impending doom when the trumpeter had played the notes that sent his company up over the ladders into a hell of barbed wire, tear gas, and blood.

The mouth of the fireplace seemed to grow larger until the opening stood higher than a man. One by one, with Louisa leading the way, each princess stepped through the fireplace and disappeared.

He stood gaping for a moment. He had thought he could no longer be astonished by magic, not after he'd seen an old woman grow young and a pack that never wanted for food. He stood for so long that nearly all the princesses had crossed over before he found his wits again. Racing over so he would not be left behind, his cloak brushed against the last princess as they crossed the threshold together.

"What was that?" little Elise asked, looking around but not seeing him. "Did anyone else feel that?"

"Feel what?" Mary asked.

"A soft brush as I came through the portal." Elise rubbed her arm as if still feeling his cloak's touch. "It was as if I'd been joined by a ghost."

"Perhaps Mother has finally come to right her wrong." The bitterness in Louisa's tone could not be missed, and the soldier wondered at the remark.

He followed the sisters through a winding cave illuminated by glowing trees. Though the trunks gave off the light, the leaves appeared to be made of various precious metals with gemstone fruits. He pulled a ruby apple off one tree taking a few golden leaves with it. Elise spun around when the apple snapped from the branch, but he stuffed the apple in his cloak before she could see. Eyes narrowed, the girl searched the area behind her but found nothing.

They came out of the cave, and he stifled a gasp. He

had thought that the Southern Front was Hell. He had been wrong. The Southern Front had been humankind's attempt to recreate Hell on Earth. Despite their best efforts, humankind had failed.

Nothing could have prepared him for the landscape he stood in now. The women marched down a beach covered not in sand, but the broken bones of some type of small animal. For once he wished he hadn't been quite so interested in science; otherwise, he might not have been able to label things like the vertebrae and clavicles scattered on the ground. He tried not to gag as his own steps crunched the bones as if he trod through a pile of fallen leaves.

The bone beach ran down to an underground lake covered in patches of fire. At times, pockets of air above the lake would also catch fire in bursts of light and roars of sound that might have been beautiful if they weren't so terrifying. The air was filled with the rot of decay and the smell of not so fresh eggs that have been left too long in the sun.

He wanted to run howling back into the cave and back to the woods. He wanted to throw himself at the feet of the witch and cry that he was right and she was wrong and he wasn't brave enough to save these girls from whatever lived over the burning waters. He wanted to do a number of things, but instead he stood, hiding in his cloak, and watched the twelve princesses prepare for war.

They formed a loose half circle with the youngest princess in the middle. Louisa and Mary stood at the center of the arc while the twins knelt on either side, planting their various quivers in the ground. Mary held a collapsible spyglass up to her eye.

"Nothing in the air," she reported to her sisters. "It looks like it's just foot soldiers in the boats this evening. Berith appears to be in command again."

"Wonderful," muttered one of the older sisters. She tossed her sword from one hand to the other but otherwise showed none of the nerves she surely felt.

"It wouldn't be a real battle without the Grand Duke of Hell," said Louisa. "You all weren't hoping for one of the easy skirmishes we have when Berith doesn't attend, were you?"

Grim chuckles answered her.

"There's something odd," said Mary. "There's a large white boat following Berith's. It's almost twice the size of the others."

"Let me see." Louisa peered through the glass.

The soldier could tell the moment Louisa spotted the unexpected ship. Already tense, her body seemed to stiffen into a block of stone. She unfroze enough to lower the spyglass, but even that movement seemed slowed by her body's unwillingness to move.

"We are being graced with his Lordship's presence this evening."

All the women began to murmur, and Elise shrank back so much she nearly collided with the soldier where he stood behind her still hidden by his cloak.

He didn't know for sure who the Lord of this place was although he had a very good idea. He stepped around Elise, placing another barrier (even if it was invisible) between the littlest princess and whatever sailed towards them on that boat.

"They're coming," Mary warned.

The women grew silent and held their various weapons at the ready. The twins aimed their bows, and Louisa loaded her revolvers. The rest stood their ground with a grim determination he found nearly as unsettling as their environment. He hadn't anything other than a dulled pocket knife, but he drew it and crouched before little Elise, ready to join the princesses in their desperate stand.

"Steady," said Louisa, but her words weren't needed. No one wept or lost their nerve. In silence they waited.

Mary had raised her spyglass again. She cocked her head to the side for a moment and then peered through it once more. "That's odd."

"Odder than Lucifer personally gracing us with his presence?"

Mary shot Louisa a look the soldier couldn't interpret. "Lord Lucifer appears to be holding a white handkerchief," said Mary. "He waves it at me every time I look his way."

"Better and better." Louisa dropped her head back and sighed as if praying to the Heavens for patience. "Since I doubt he wishes to surrender, he must want to talk." She looked around at her sisters. "Stay on your guard, and no one, I mean no one," she looked pointedly back at Elise, "makes a sound. He will twist and turn your words until you have agreed to the opposite of what you wish. Let me do the talking."

Around the half circle, heads nodded, but no one relaxed their fighting stance.

The boats pulled up and ground onto the bone beach. Demon and fell beasts of all manner climbed from the boats, but they remained at the shore. A tall knight rode off the lead boat on a horse the color of congealed blood. The knight stood at the head of the demon army, but they made no move to attack.

The larger boat came into view, but it did not pull up to the shore. Instead, Lucifer proved he had no need to disembark. One moment the fifty feet between the princesses and the demon horde stood empty, the next a breathtaking, beautiful slip of a man stood before them. The soldier's jaw fell open. He had been expecting a red entity with cloven hooves and a pointed tail. At the very least horns should have sprouted from Lucifer's head. This man looked like he had once been a classical sculpture a lustful god had brought to life.

Louisa appeared unmoved, and behind the soldier Elise whimpered, but the rest of the princesses stood as if stunned by his beauty. One girl reached out as if drawn to him, while another took a step forward.

"Hold," Louisa said, breaking the spell Lucifer had woven over her sisters. Weapons came back up, and the women once again became resolved. "He's only a man of sorts," she added.

"Only a great deal lovelier," said Lucifer.

Louisa shifted her weight, clearly put out, but she said nothing.

"You needn't chastise," said the Devil as if she'd

spoken her disapproval aloud. "It's not as if I lie. Besides, vain and pride are two of my favorite sins." He treated them to a smile that dazzled in that underground pit and promised of pleasures unknown in the mortal realm. "Not my absolute favorite though." He licked his lips. It wasn't a suggestive movement, yet it suggested things to the soldier all the same. He was obscurely disappointed that the Devil's tongue hadn't proved to be forked. Had the clergy gotten nothing right?

Her sisters might shift uncomfortably, but Louisa was unmoved. "Your Majesty." She greeted him with a small but respectful dip of her head, one royal to another. "To what do we owe this honor?"

"There is a new player on the field," said Lucifer. He gave a small shiver as if delighted by the prospect. "I came to greet him and collect my winnings."

Louisa turned to look back at Elise, and the soldier was struck by the horror, and fear, on her face.

"I don't understand," said Louisa, her calm assurance lost. Her hands shook, knocking the revolvers against her legs. "There is no new player."

All of the sisters looked around and at one another in confusion with the undercurrent of fear growing stronger.

Lucifer sighed as if he had just experienced the most delicate caress. "Oh, but this is delightful. Perhaps you don't realize he's here. Is it possible you can't see him?"

With the Devil clearly able to see him, the soldier saw no point in concealing his presence any longer. He drew back the cloak and pulled down the hood.

"Oh no," muttered Elise from behind.

The sisters turned almost as one, and their shocked dismay could be felt through the heat of Hell. Mary started to move to him, but Louisa held her back.

"You," Louisa said. The word was innocuous enough, but he flinched as if she'd uttered the vilest of curses. She turned back to the Devil. "We did not bring him nor seek out his help. We have told no one just as you and I once agreed." Like Lucifer, the soldier could hear the note of pleading in her voice, and it appalled him that a woman once so proud could sound so small.

"And yet he's here." The Devil rubbed his hands together like a villain in the silent films they used to show in town before the start of the war. "All of your souls are mine."

The princesses' despair was written in every line of every body. Louisa tried to rally, but he could tell from her voice that she knew it was a lost cause. "We did not seek his aid. We did not tell him of the pact."

"It's true," the soldier said, surprising everyone, including himself. "They have neither sought my aid, nor have I offered it. I'm not sure what agreement you brokered, but if the princesses were to forfeit their souls if they sought help, then they have not forfeited them now."

"You stand there with knife drawn," drawled Lucifer, waving at the puny pocket knife still clutched in the soldier's hand. "You cannot have me believe you didn't mean to protect these girls."

"These women need no protection of mine," he said pointing out an obvious truth. He gestured at their weapons. "I saw an approaching horde of demons and thought only of myself," he only half-lied. "I am a coward. Ask anyone in my village."

The Devil seemed to flicker as if he were dividing his corporeal self between many points of time. "You are certainly not held in high esteem. Your cowardly reputation bears you out as does the princesses' surprise to find you here." Lucifer sulked for a moment. "Fine. I suppose the agreement was not broken. You may continue to fight for the youngest," he said to Louisa. "But you," he pointed at the soldier, "you may not interfere."

"I will not lift my knife in their aid," the soldier promised. He folded the knife back up and shoved it back in his pocket. "This is clearly not my fight, and I do not fight for what I do not understand."

"What a charitable way to look at the desertion of your post." Lucifer gave him a snide smile, but the soldier realized there was truth in the Devil's words despite the intent to wound. The soldier had never been comfortable with a war fought for inches of land or for the chance for one nation to prove their technology superior to another. He had resented aiming a rifle at boys like him only born on the opposite side of an imaginary line. The war still felt as wrong on his 428th day on the frontline as it had back when he had refused to enlist. Could it have been more than cowardice that had led him away from the Southern Front and a war he found repugnant?

"I will honor our original agreement," Lucifer said again to Louisa, "the one which modified the contract signed by your mother."

Behind the soldier Elise groaned, and several of the princesses seemed to sag for a moment. They quickly marshalled their strength when Lucifer made a quick motion with two fingers on his right hand. The demon horde on the shore began to move forward.

"What contract?" the soldier asked.

"None of your business," snapped Louisa. "We cannot have your aid."

"Still not offering it," the soldier snapped back. "I asked what contract, Your Majesty," he called again to Lucifer.

Lucifer paused and made another gesture with his hand. The horde stopped advancing.

"Curious, aren't you?" he said, raking the soldier with a long glance that seemed to take in every inch of the man from the inside out. "Curiosity, such a dangerous sin."

The soldier shrugged, unsure how to answer.

"Very well." Lucifer struck a pose like an orator in a painting about classical antiquity. "Once upon a time, a beautiful, yet naïve woman found herself queen of a small mountain kingdom. She wished to present her king with an heir, but month after month went by without a child."

"It was only six months," muttered Louisa. "She was a fool."

"Well." Mary shifted her head back and forth as if the ideas inside were waffling and couldn't decide which way to go. "Mother's generation wasn't taught biological basics like we were. She might not have known how conception works."

"She made a deal with the Devil. She was a fool."

Mary couldn't argue that and didn't. The soldier began to understand the source of Louisa's bitterness.

"Ladies." Lucifer glared at them like a petulant child. "A master storyteller is weaving his words." He made a gesture. Both Louisa and Mary opened their mouths, but no sound came out. "Better."

Lucifer resumed his pose. "Months went by without a child, and the queen became increasingly desperate. She consulted soothsayers, physicians, and wise women from throughout the land. Finally, an old but kind looking woman was brought before her." Lucifer dropped his pose for a moment and stage whispered, "Spoiler alert. That old woman was me."

"Spoiler?" mouthed Mary. Louisa shrugged, and the soldier too wondered what the Devil had meant.

"The old woman held the queen's hand and shook her head in a mournful manner. She broke the news of the queen's barrenness as gently as she could, but the queen still wailed in anguish at the woman's words.

"The old woman was moved by the queen's tears

and offered her a small potion known to cure all ills including those affecting the womb."

Louisa snorted, and even the soldier had troubled believing Lucifer had ever been emotionally affected by anything.

"The queen reached for the potion, desperate for the potential children it might bring, but the old woman held it just out of her royal grasp.

"'My dear,' the old woman told the queen. 'Nothing, not even children, are given for free.' I, I mean, the old woman pulled out a contract ready for the queen's signature. 'With this potion you will have more children then you have ever dreamed, and in return, all I require is the company of the last born.'

"The queen was desperate, yet she hesitated. To consign her unborn young to such a vague pact filled her with concern. She negotiated with the old woman until a clause was added to the pact. Should someone in a selfless act offer to take the child's place, the child would be spared."

"She planned to offer herself, didn't she?" the soldier asked, wondering what had gone wrong.

"Probably." Lucifer shrugged and dropped his pose. "She never had the chance."

"And who's fault is that?" Louisa shouted out. She looked as surprised as anyone to discover she could speak again.

"Not mine," Lucifer said, looking bored. "I kept up my end of the bargain. She had a whole passel full of brats. I can't help that it finally did her in. Childbirth is always risky."

The soldier glanced back at Elise, still standing behind him. The little girl didn't cower, but stood her ground, holding her small dagger in the same defiant manner as her older sisters held their swords.

"And none of you offered to take her place?" The soldier stared at the princesses expecting to meet faces filled with shame and regret. Instead, each girl gazed at him with the same steady stare they had used before.

"None of us are cowardly enough for such an act," said Mary in a quiet voice.

The soldier stared at her for a moment. Like the folks back home, he would have considered the act one of bravery not cowardice.

"Cowardly?" asked the Devil.

Louisa snorted. "He doesn't understand. What a surprise." She turned to answer Lucifer, but from the way Mary stared at the soldier, he suspected Louisa really spoke to him.

"Yes, cowardly. For how would we choose who to sacrifice? Who would we not miss if someone were to go in Elise's place? Each of my sisters is as dear to me as the next, and I would suffer equally no matter who was consigned to your vile realm. I need them, and they need me."

"And our country needs its heir," said Mary in a low voice.

Louisa reached over and squeezed Mary's hand, but otherwise didn't answer her. Instead, she continued to stare at the Devil. "That is why that night, the night of our mother's death, when you and your henchman snuck into our rooms to steal away my six year old sister, I followed and fought." She pointed at the duke on his demon horse, and the knight nodded in acknowledgement of that night. "And that is why I begged and struck my own foolish deal with the Devil. Each night my sisters and I would risk injury and even death fighting for my youngest sister and her soul. We would fight alone and outnumbered with no hope of aid lest we forfeit our own souls. In return, for each night we stayed standing, we earned another day where Elise could not be taken."

"Foolish child," said the Devil. He shrugged. "I have always thought so. You are young and strong now, but what happens when you weaken with age, when your hands become too gnarled to hold a sword? One day you will fall, and the youngest will be mine. It's only a matter of time, and I have all eternity."

"Perhaps," said Louisa. She didn't sag or in any way show that his words had wounded her. If anything, she sounded even more determined than she had before. "But my sisters and I will give her as many days as we can."

The princesses cheered, and behind the soldier, Elise shouted a battle cry.

The soldier stared at the women arrayed around him and realized that here he saw more courage before him than he had ever witnessed on the Southern Front. These women fought for their cause and what they believed was right every night. Perhaps that was true courage—doing what was right even when others doubted you. Perhaps it was braver to fight every night for a sister instead of sacrificing yourself in her place. Perhaps it was braver to walk away from a war than to continue fighting for something you never thought was right in the first place.

For the first time since the day the war had begun, the soldier felt lighter as if the weight of cowardice had lifted from his shoulders. Enlisting and fighting in a war he hadn't believed in, that had been the work of a coward. It had been months since he had walked away. He hadn't been a coward, not really, in a very long time.

The soldier gave a small chuckle and stood straighter than he ever had while standing at attention before his superior officers. The old woman had been right. The princesses had saved him from himself, and in return, he would save them from the Devil.

"I sacrifice myself in their place," he said. The soldier had meant to sound grand like a hero in a myth, but his pronouncement fell flat. No one seemed to notice he had spoken. He had thought himself a coward for years, and that kind of thinking isn't overcome in a matter of moments no matter how powerful the epiphany that prompts the change in view.

He cleared his throat and tried again. "I sacrifice myself in their place."

"What?" asked Lucifer. Mary gasped. They had heard him this time.

"You heard." The soldier pushed past the line of women and walked until he was within a few feet of the

Devil before stopping. "I offer myself in Elise's place."

"No," cried Mary.

The soldier smiled but didn't turn back.

"Oh, don't get your petticoats in a twist," Lucifer said to Mary even though she still wore breeches and there wasn't a petticoat in sight. "He can't interfere or I get all of your souls. He agreed to that earlier."

"I agreed to not raise my knife in their defense. I have certainly not done so. Their souls are still their own."

"You ..." Lucifer's mouth snapped shut. "Well, damn. I hate it when it comes down to wording." He tapped a single finger against his lips in a slow, constant manner the soldier found almost hypnotic. "Your souls are still safe," he said to the princesses, dropping his hand back to his side. "Apparently, this is just not my night."

The soldier didn't turn around, but a gentle breeze caressed the back of his neck as if twelve women had exhaled in relief all at once.

"But is this a truly selfless act?" asked Lucifer. He circled the soldier caressing him with a gaze as sharp as nails. Lucifer trailed a finger across the soldier's back from shoulder blade to shoulder blade, and the soldier shivered, not entirely from fear. "It's true I don't see how you benefit," the Devil continued, "but is any act truly selfless?"

The soldier didn't reply.

"You do realize you will be spending an eternity in Hell, the realm of torture and despair, seeing to my every pleasure." Lucifer smiled, and it was all the soldier could do to keep from screaming in terror. The Devil's smile promised that his pleasure would result in only torment for the soldier.

"Yes," the soldier managed to spit out through chattering teeth. He had never felt such fear, and yet he knew this was what he needed to do. The realization that in this manner he was braver than anyone could ever have anticipated brought him an unexpected sense of peace. He might be history's greatest fool, but he wasn't a coward.

"I will flay your body into little pieces, reassemble them, and do it again." The Devil continued along in this vein for quite some time with each torture he described more gruesome than the one before. At one point one of the princesses retched at one of Lucifer's more visceral descriptions. The list became so long and so ludicrous that the soldier became bored, and then he became curious.

"Yes, yes, a thousand times yes." The soldier interrupted a rather ridiculous torture involving hummingbirds and eight week old kittens. "You're going to do unspeakable things to me, and I still agree to take Elise's place. Just why are you trying to talk me out of it?"

"Because I don't want you," Lucifer shrieked. He stomped his foot and sulked like a spoiled child denied a favorite toy. "And if I take you, I can't have one of them, and if I don't take you, I still can't have one of them because the contract only stipulates a selfless act. It doesn't say by whom."

"Pity," said Louisa. She came to stand next to the soldier. Mary joined him on the other side and rested one of her hands on his arm. "Then I suppose you have a decision to make," said Louisa, using the voice of a future queen. "Will you take him or not?"

Lucifer stood until he was within an inch of the soldier's face. He stared deep into the soldier's eyes, and the man could feel the Devil reading his very soul.

"Take him away," Lucifer said to Louisa. "There's no point in my keeping him here. He realizes he's no longer a coward, and nothing I can do to him would even come close to the torment he has already inflicted on himself." He turned to the soldier. "You're no fun."

Mary pulled on the soldier's arm, and they both took a step back.

"The contract has been completed?" asked Louisa, standing her ground. The soldier and Mary took another step backward. "You relinquish your claim on Elise? All of us, including the soldier, still retain our souls?"

"Yes." Lucifer waved a hand, dismissing them. When Louisa still didn't move, he added, "You might want to run now before I set my pets on you just for fun." He waved at the demon horde still gathered on the beach. "I'm not in the best mood, you know."

All of them turned and scrambled for the cave, the bones of the beach crunching underfoot in their mad dash to get away. The soldier chanced one glance back. Lucifer still sulked on the beach and kicked a demon that dared to come too close. He didn't order his army to give chase though. He seemed finished with them all, at least for now.

In the morning, the King had the doors unlocked only to find his daughters well-rested with shoes only slightly scuffed, with intact soles not worn through to the inner linings. The soldier sat chatting with Mary about an article she had read in a natural history magazine. If the king was surprised to find his daughters cheerful for the first time in years, he didn't show it. He merely demanded an explanation.

Louisa, Mary, and the soldier took him to one side and in low voices explained about the contract, the Devil, and the nightly battles the women had endured. The king was skeptical at first, but the soldier brought out the ruby apple with solid gold leaves he had pulled off the tree in the cave. The younger girls pulled out their sabres to demonstrate their fighting skills, and the twins showed off their archery by shooting at pillows from across the length of the throne room, much to the court's horror.

By the noontime meal, even the most doubtful of the king's advisors agreed that the mystery had been solved. When one night, and then two, and then a month of them had passed without a return of Lucifer or his demon hordes, even Louisa was convinced that the soldier had helped them outwit the Devil for good. She was less convinced that she needed to marry a mere boy who had not yet reached his majority.

The soldier and Mary were also not convinced of the soundness of the plan. Between the three of them, they managed to convince the king that such a reward was unwelcome to all the parties involved. The soldier agreed that becoming a duke with a small estate not far from Adventia would be reward enough. He enrolled in the Helvetti University and convinced the king to enroll Princess Mary with him. While the war continued to rage on the rest of continent, he and Mary debated and experimented in the University's labs.

He considered going to tell the witch of his success, but he suspected she knew. One night, he had returned to his rooms in the palace to find the cloak missing. He assumed the witch had come to reclaim it and perhaps give it to some other traveler in need. After all, he was now a scholarly duke with a betrothal to Princess Mary soon to be announced, not a soul-sick soldier escaping from his past. With his promise to the witch fulfilled and a princess by his side, it was time for the new duke to push away the past and pursue his own happily ever after.

Madeline Smoot is the publisher of CBAY Books and former Editorial Director for Children's Books of Blooming Tree Press. In other words, Madeline knows a lot about publishing and the process of bringing a book to market. She holds an MA in Children's Literature from Hollins University and loves bringing together new stories—especially those that involve fairy tales and their tropes. Madeline lives in Dallas, Texas, with her husband, son, a dog, and more books than should fit in any normal person's house.